eSPEC BOOKS

IN A FLASH
2020

Christopher J. Burke

eSpec Books
Pennsville, NJ

PUBLISHED BY
eSpec Books LLC
Danielle McPhail,
Publisher
PO Box 242,
Pennsville, New Jersey 08070
www.especbooks.com

ISBN: 978-1-949691-43-6
ISBN (ebook): 978-1-949691-42-9

Copy Editor: Greg Schauer
Cover Art and Design: Mike McPhail, McP Digital Graphics
Interior Design: Danielle McPhail

To my wife, Antoinette.

CONTENTS

FANTASY

FAMILIAR FEELING

DIANA SAT IN LINE WITH HER CLASSMATES ON THE GREAT LAWN IN front of the Academy's main entrance. A row of ceremonial torches lined the path at the lawn's edge. To their right, the woods and the road into town. To the left, the path down to the shimmering lake, reflecting the mountains beyond. Above, the sky darkened as evening encroached with the sun setting behind them.

She could hardly contain her excitement. It was the first day of the second month of the third term of school. The full complement of four-and-twenty sophomores of the Carrowmore School for Magic and Wizardry wore their new black robes. Black was the color for "wise fools." They would wear these robes for the rest of the year. But today, through hard work, determination, and a little bit of luck, each might get an assistant for their studies. And not just for this semester, but maybe for a lifetime.

When the sun set and the teachers lit the torches, Diana and her classmates would attempt to summon their first familiars.

She contemplated the collection of stones that lay before her. In *Mystical Geology*, they learned the elemental properties of different types of rocks. Forged in fire. Shaped by water. Air trapped within. They had learned how best to polish and cut them to maximize their magical potential. Even something as small as a pebble could unleash immense power when properly crushed to a powder and mixed into a potion.

On their first day at Carrowmore, each student received a stone from a member of the senior class. Diana treasured the onyx she received from Kaara, her Big Sister, at her induction ceremony. Over the following year, she'd collect, reject, and replace so many more in preparation for this day. Now each young lad and lady sat on their heels on the grass, with their wands on their laps. They had their most perfect assortments piled before them—gifts from Mother Earth, pieces of her own essence.

Diana looked at Lena to her left, and Thomas to her right. They each exchanged nervous smiles and shrugs. She noticed that Thomas had a collection that was almost exclusively volcanic, with a polished piece of marble as a catalyst. "I'm hoping for something fire-based," he whispered. Lena said she heard that someone was using some fossil rocks for extra "oomph." Diana hoped that wasn't true because it could backfire badly.

Anxiously, they awaited the command from Professor Caoimhe, whose name Diana learned to pronounce "Kee-va," after saying it incorrectly on the first day of class. On her signal, all students would, with great care and precision, place the fist-sized stones in a circle in front of them.

The professor stepped forward, away from the other teachers taking part in the ceremony. She looked at the orange tones in the sky above the school's gables. "You have approximately fifteen minutes to finish your circle. Consider and reconsider each placement. If you fail tonight, you will have to wait until the spring to try again."

In their *Arithmagic* studies, Diana learned that the Roman word for pebble was calculus, and they would manipulate those pebbles on an abacus. That's where they got the word 'ca*lculate.*' And now she had to calculate where she would place her stones.

The professor looked to her left and then to her right, and saw all the students at attention, afraid to even breathe. Then she uttered the most powerful word: "Begin."

Stones fell from their mounds and popped out of hands as eager students raced to complete the task in front of them. Diana ignored them as she reverently placed Kaara's onyx first. It may have been the least potent in her collection, but its emotional connection compensated for what it lacked in raw power.

No one knew what kind of animal—or being—that they might summon. But it seemed to Diana that every other student had a desire of some kind.

Some wanted a creature of great power or prestige, even if it needed to be raised from a cub. Some wanted something that said, "I am strong" or "I am fierce," even if it wasn't of magical origin. The more practical hoped for something that would help with their magical specialization. They didn't have to declare until later in the year, but many already had an inkling.

Diana was the odd duck in the row. She wasn't sure what she wanted to study yet. She'd spoken to her counselor, who told her that feelings of uncertainty were normal.

There was one other wizard in her family. Her Uncle Billy. He was a ranger in the Forest Service. His familiar was a brown bear named Boo Boo. Diana remembered nuzzling it when she was just a toddler and it was a cub. Uncle Billy said he could feel her warmth through the bear. That's how he knew she'd be a wizard one day and have a great friend like Boo.

But he would laugh about how embarrassed he was back in school when he first summoned a squirrel. "Everyone said it was because I'm a nut."

Whatever appeared, Diana knew it would be okay. At least, she hoped it would.

But she was getting ahead of herself. First, she had to make something appear.

Teachers and counselors walked back and forth, making helpful suggestions. *Did you mean to put those two gneiss together? Are you sure you want basalt next to that shale?* While the students had to pass or fail on their own, no one wanted anyone to be disappointed. Head of Guidance, Madame Dovenna, addressed the assembled pupils. This ceremony had to be taken very seriously, as it formed a lasting commitment. She asked the students if they were prepared for all the responsibilities that would follow. If anyone didn't feel ready, this was the time to back out.

None did.

Thomas leaned toward Diana. "How long of a commitment will it really be? Most of us will summon mundane animals that will die within the next five years or so."

The student to his right shushed him. "Do you plan on not taking care of it?"

Madame Dovenna smiled and nodded to Professor Caoimhe, who addressed her class. "Then, let us commence!"

The professor lifted her arms as a raven dropped from the sky to land on her shoulder. Faculty members retrieved and lit their torches as she began to chant. They fell into line and joined the chorus. None of this was part of the actual summoning ceremony, except to focus positive energy from the flames, the air, and the earth, and the trees, the lake, and the mountains.

Diana concentrated. Since she woke this morning, she'd gone over the procedure dozens of times in her mind. She'd worked through the steps. But a dance is more than just memorizing where to place your feet. She had to feel the astral melody, sway with the ethereal rhythm. She ignored the flashes of light about her and concentrated on her own circle of stones. Her incantation ended with a flourish of her wand and a snap of her wrist. Next came a blinding flash. The force of it knocked her backward.

Lying on her back, Diana saw two birds taking to the sky and heard cries of "Wait! Come back!" She listened to the commotion and the sounds of surprise and disappointment. Then came the caws, squeaks, chirps, yaps, meows, hisses, and bleats.

Up and down the line, a few classmates were also blown back by their invocations. One had broken his circle with an unfortunate kick. Another girl was on her hands and knees, trying to replace stones, crying, pleading. Counselors moved in to offer support.

In her friends' circles, she saw an assortment of the usual mundane creatures, cats and birds, a few rats and snakes. She saw that someone managed to summon a sprite or a pixie. *Was it a gnome?*

Diana was afraid to look at her own circle, afraid even to move. Apprehension filled more of her than curiosity. Then she felt something against her foot. Had she broken the seal when she'd fallen? She didn't hear anything and didn't want to look.

Lena shouted, "Diana! What's that?"

That made Diana bolt upright. She stared in disbelief. In the center of her stone circle lay an egg. It was blue, like a robin's but ten times as large.

Diana reached forward, then stopped. She hesitated with her hands just shy of touching the shell. She thought she could feel ripples of energy flowing from the egg. Frozen, she barely noticed footsteps running across the lawn or the sudden torchlight above her.

"Pick it up, Diana," Professor Caoimhe said in hushed tones. "Carefully."

Her trance broken, Diana scooped up the egg and nestled it in both hands. It was warm to the touch. More than that, this was a warmth that washed over her, filled her body. She'd never felt anything like it before. Not even with Boo Boo.

An older, bearded wizard joined them. Professor Droelean had been the head of the school's Aviculture Studies for decades. "What do we have here?"

Diana offered the egg to him. He held up a hand in protest. "It's important that *you* hold it now. Vital."

He adjusted his glasses and peered more closely. "I haven't seen one of these since I was a mere stripling. Congratulations, young lady. That is a dragon egg, although I'm not certain at the moment just what kind it may be. It's going to require a lot of attention until it hatches." He paused and thought about it. "Even more afterward. We'll work with your counselor to arrange a schedule."

Just then, a dove flew overhead. Professor Droelean excused himself to help its owner.

The egg felt both warmer and heavier in her hands. Diana had a horrifying thought and looked up at Prossefor Caoimhe. "Will its mother come looking for it?"

Her teacher smiled. "Were its mother still alive, you wouldn't have been able to call it here. Not with the bonds dragons have. You likely rescued it."

Diana was about to lean forward to set the egg down. Instead, she sat back and cradled the egg against her body. She had a sudden revelation: bonds! That's what the warmth she felt was. A new bond forming. Then she realized one more thing.

Everything would definitely be more than just okay.

THE SECOND-STORY JOB

"THREE ROGUES WALK INTO A TAVERN... STOP ME IF YOU'VE HEARD THIS one before."

Koppig stopped, one hand on the swinging door. He looked back over his shoulder. "We all heard it before, Roda. Last week. When we walked into the last tavern."

Her mouth twisted with bitter thoughts. "Exactly. How'd things go there?"

The bald man pushed past them and glanced about the room. "Will you two ladies quit your squabbling?"

"Only one's a lady, Zoeker. And he's standing right behind you."

Koppig ignored them. "It wasn't my fault. That wasn't a proper inn. Some farmer brews a batch from his still and hangs a lantern for the neighbors. Horrible stuff, mind you. And did you notice that they were all paying with grains and roots and vegetables?"

Roda remembered well enough. "So, you decided to rob his house?"

"I just peeked into the master bedroom. There was no need for him to come at me with that hot poker."

"There was more of a need for that than for the wife to come at *me* with the butcher knife, screaming her flippin' head about 'hospitality'!"

Zoeker finished surveying the main hall before them. "Both of you shut up."

Koppig's need to get in the last word won out. "Just saying, dumb little podunk hamlet."

The leader corralled his companions, grabbing one by his ponytail and the other, gently, by her upper arm, which was as far as he'd push his luck. "Well, this town isn't 'podunk.' Let's take it easy here. Our pouches are full. We can eat and drink, shop and spend, like regular folks for an evening or two. Pick up some supplies and new equipment, and maybe get a few leads for our next stop. It would be nice, for a change, not to have to run out in the middle of the night."

Koppig batted the hand from his hair. He met the stares of each of his partners and then scanned the crowd. "Fine. But I see my mark for the night."

Following his line of sight, Roda spotted a well-dressed lady with a chain about her neck holding a gold locket, which was nestled comfortably in an overly ample bosom. "Are you settin' your sights on the lady or the locket?"

He shrugged. "I'll settle for either. But with our new rules, I'll have to wait a day for the locket."

Roda threw her head back to laugh. "If you get her, skip the locket. Take the wedding band and the diamond. She won't be needin' them anymore."

Koppig looked again. "Ooh, a challenge. Now I'm more interested." Without another word, he slipped away into the crowd and across the room.

The other two moved to a corner away from the door. Roda looked about. "And what's your game for the evening? Need me to find you some companionship?"

"I already have you."

"You'll have better luck with that robed monk over there."

"Yes, I've heard that about the clergy in these parts. Still, you and I will likely be sharing a bed tonight."

"Aye. All three of us in one room, in one big bed, most likely. From the size of this crowd, we'll be lucky if we get a private room to ourselves for what we can spare. But you'll be missing a hand in the mornin' if it wanders in your sleep. Or any part that touches me." She caressed the hilt of her dagger for emphasis.

He grinned. "That's the least amount of violence you've threatened this month. I'm wearing you down. Don't worry. I know not to try anything."

"You know that now, but will you remember it after your third tankard of mead?"

"Mead, yes. I could go for some mead. Haven't had a proper drink in weeks." With that, he started off.

"Where are you going? The bar is this way."

"To try my luck with the monk, of course. They're holy fonts of information. They know their spirits well. And when those spirits fill them, they tend to spill some valuable information. So first, I'll get him to tell me what I should be drinking. And then, with luck, by the time I stumble into bed, I should have leads on our next job."

With that, Zoeker melded into the crowd.

Roda was happy with the prospect of a moment alone to let her hair down and shake the dust out of it. Those long red locks obscured her vision and muffled her hearing just long enough to allow someone to approach unnoticed.

"Traveling with your brothers?"

Spinning around quickly, she moved a hand to her dagger. The well-dressed gentleman saw the motion and took a step back, careful not to spill his drink.

She swept her hair back and regained her composure. Inspecting the man, she noted his height, build, and equanimity. Deciding to see how this played out, she tilted her head a little and smiled. "They're not my brothers."

He raised an eyebrow, along with the corner of his lip. "No?"

"They're, er, more like young uncles."

"Quite young, it seems."

"Grandpa didn't know when to quit, the Father and Mother rest him." She briefly folded her arms, hands to each shoulder, to honor the Duality. The gentleman returned the gesture, still mindful of his drink, and gave a slight nod of his head. "Story is that Grandma helped him to quit. And the milkmaid as well."

"The milkmaid? Any relation to your young 'uncles'?"

Roda glanced toward her two escorts. "I can recognize a jest, but others might not. You ought to be careful. You wouldn't be as pretty a gentleman were you a foot shorter. 'Twould be a pity."

"'Pretty,' am I?"

Roda blushed a moment, then gave him a second look. He was well-groomed and well-mannered, with expensive rings on both hands. A mark? Or a pleasant evening? She started to regret her earlier admonishments to Koppig, but tomorrow would be another day. She was still working out her options when she realized he was speaking to her.

"Allow me to introduce myself. My name is Chapman, but I travel under the name Pennywhistle, an unrepentant, itinerant tradesman."

A traveling merchant? Possibly a mark *and* a pleasant evening. She nearly sang out, "Roda."

"Forgive my manners, Roda. You obviously just came off the road. You must be parched. Allow me to fetch you some wine. I'm also in need of another ale."

Wine sounded good, so long as it was only wine. "No need to fetch. I'll walk with you." Might the merchant mix in a potable of his own? Or maybe have a deal with the barman?

As it turned out, the overworked barmaid barely gave either of them more notice than required to pour a goblet of red wine and draw a flagon of ale. All the tables were filled with travelers and townsfolk eating and drinking, boasting and gambling.

Chapman nodded his head toward the door. "Care to step outside. Drink under the stars?"

Roda's eyes narrowed at the suggestion, trying to read his face and body language. There were many possible reasons to be outside, away from the crowd, many of which were distasteful. Of course, there were more than a few that were not. However, she had both her dagger and her agility if she needed to defend or evade. She hoped sating her curiosity wouldn't involve someone getting stabbed in the back.

"Lead the way." A moment later, she was taking a sip of wine in the night air.

The merchant hoisted his ale, draining more than half of it, then wiped the back of his hand across his mouth. He seemed hesitant to look at Roda or even speak. Finally, he turned to her. "I have a proposition for you. I'm sure it'll be worth your while."

And there it was. One backstabbing, coming up. "I'm not some tavern whore."

All good humor left Chapman's face. His tone grew sharp. "No. You're a thief. That was obvious the moment the three of you walked in. But you were the one I thought could best help me. I need something…recovered."

She kept her distance from him, out of arm's reach. "You lost something? And you want me to steal it back? If I were what you think I am, I'd need more details."

He finished his ale. "Fair enough. A bad mix of ale and games of chance last night cost me a fair amount of coin. I also lost an amulet, an heirloom given to me by my father. I need that back."

Roda scoffed, "You want me to retrieve your gambling losses? Wouldn't be worth my effort."

"No," his voice was quiet, measured. "I've lost more money than that before gaming, both fair and rigged. And have won just as much. A few coins foolishly lost don't matter to me. But the amulet is another matter. I offered a fair price to buy it back and was rebuffed. And it was a rigged game, so it was basically stolen from me. My first hope was to pay a ransom. The next step is to hire a thief."

It seemed too elaborate to be a setup. Not in a town like this. Would anyone need much of a reason to hang a thief? Or even proof? "Okay, so this amulet was stolen from you. If I'm a thief, as you say, why would I steal from another one? Professional courtesy and all that."

He looked her straight in the eyes. "Did I mention that there were six others in this game, some of whom lost more money than I? It would all be ripe for taking."

The pot had been raised, but Roda remained skeptical. "And you wouldn't want any of that loot for yourself?"

He didn't even shrug. "Their money was never mine, and I have no need of it. You are welcome to whatever you find. But we need to hurry."

"Why?"

"Because we passed him playing inside, and he's already winning. I followed him last night, so I know where he sleeps. He doesn't have the amulet on him now. It will be in the room he rents, along with other considerations for yourself."

Chapman put down his empty cup and started down the street without waiting for an answer.

"Well, I wanted to see how this played out." She looked at her wine, thought better of it, and put the goblet down. What a waste. She hurried after the merchant.

They didn't have far to walk when they came to a row of houses just off the main road. Their target had a room on the second floor at the back of a house near the end of the street. Access could be gained through a window in the narrow lane between buildings. Perfect for someone small and agile, Roda realized. That's why Chapman had approached her and not Koppig or Zoeker.

It was an easy climb. Her dagger helped slide the window open effortlessly. Once inside, she listened in the dark before deciding that it was safe enough to light the candle on the table. The room looked sparse, as if someone poor lived here, someone not worth robbing. But it didn't take long to discover that wasn't the case. She found several small stashes of money secreted about the room and a small chest under the bed. Examining it with caution, she poked and tapped it a few times with her dagger, before pulling it out. Picking locks wasn't a specialty of hers. Bashing them with the dagger's hilt compensated for that.

Inside, Roda found the amulet on top of a pile of necklaces, brooches, and rings. Quickly, she put the amulet around her neck and filled her pouch with an assortment of gems and jewelry. She filled two more purses with coins until she feared the weight would cause her to fall. Snuffing the flame, she was out the window and down in the lane by the time the candle stopped smoking.

The thief was still smiling at her good work when she heard a voice shout, "Halt! Don't move!" Not that she had a chance. For an instant, she thought she saw a crossbow bolt heading toward her head. But she felt an excruciating pain in her chest instead. Then darkness overcame her, and the ground knocked out any breath she still had in her.

❈❈

Roda expected to wake up in a cell if she woke up at all. Instead, she lay in a pile of hay, someplace dark that smelled of horses. She put her hands to her head, which hurt furiously. Then she did a quick check on the rest of her. She cursed when she realized the amulet and the bags were gone. But she still had her dagger, and she was still dressed. That was something, at least.

The stable door opened. A man, silhouetted by the moonlight, stepped in. She unsheathed her dagger despite a raging headache.

"Ah, you're awake. I hear you moving." Chapman lit a lantern and hung it on the wall. The amulet hung around his neck.

Roda held the knife in front of her in as threatening a manner as she could manage. "You have what you wanted. Where's the rest of it?"

Chapman pointed at the ground behind her. "It's buried in the hay beneath you. I didn't want anyone to find it while I went to my wagon. I went to retrieve my medical supplies. Here's something for the pain...and some water, too. You must be thirsty."

She was, but she was also confused. "How? What happened?"

He offered her the water. She put down her knife and took it. Then he held the amulet in his fingers. "My father always told me to be very protective of this little trinket, because it'll be very protective of me. His father had bartered for it with some enchantress up north many years ago. When the guard attacked, the bolt was drawn to the amulet, away from your head. But it still hit you hard enough to knock you down. You got a little bump in the fall, I'm afraid.

"With the proper incantation, the attack could have been deflected entirely. My apologies for not telling you, but I was afraid you'd realize my ransom offer might not have been as fair as I had originally suggested. As it is, I see you chose to wear it instead of stashing it in your bag. However, it turned out for the best that you did. "

Roda thought about it. Had she known, would she have just taken the amulet and fled the other way? Who could say now? The bruise would heal, and she'd come out ahead. Way ahead. Except...

"If you're wondering, the watchman who struck you fell asleep in the street before he got a look at you in that dark alley. A little powder from my ring blew his way."

Chapman helped her to her feet. She thought for a moment that he was going to make his move. Instead, he walked away, stopping at the door.

"I would say with your payment to me of this fine amulet in exchange for some valuable information, our business transaction is concluded."

Maybe it was the headache, but that sounded somewhat backward to Roda.

"Should we meet again, I am sure I'd enjoy the pleasure of your company. However, the hour is late, and I imagine your 'uncles' may be looking for you. I understand they have the room right next to mine, at the end of the hall."

And with that, the itinerant trader was gone, having completed a 'transaction.' Was that all this was? Roda gathered the bags and slowly made her way out of the stable, which was behind the inn. Looking up, she could see the window of the room at the end of the hall where Koppig and Zoeker would be. Then she saw that the window of the next room was open. She gave it some thought before deciding that despite the headache and the weight of the bags, she could scramble up the wall before Chapman got to his room.

Business was done. Anything after that was strictly personal. And he still owed her a goblet of wine.

THE LONG DUSK
OF FIOCH BRAE

L ORD BRADDAGH WOULD DIE BEFORE THIS DAY'S END. THIS MUCH WAS foretold. What no one could predict was that this day would fail to end.

My name is Atty Feirmeor, son of Dismore, the baker. That would have been my path, too, but like the promise of the next full moon, it has been denied.

The Lord of the Manor has a royal Seer. Long ago, or maybe it was just a few days, he saw the Lord's death at the end of the day after the new moon. Lord Braddagh summoned his mystics, who chanted, and sung, and screamed in tongues. And when it was done, they held the sun, the moon, and the stars in place.

The Lord threw a massive celebration that seems to last for three days, and maybe it did. People cheered in Braddagh's presence. None dared not.

And none, not advisor nor mystic, spoke of the perils that came with the endless night.

Now, the last rays of the evening sun lit the western horizon. The faintest hint, a mere sliver of the crescent moon, could be made out low in the sky. They were in exactly the same places when I started my journey down the hill from Fioch Brae. By my count, that was nearly 10,000 paces ago. I may have lost count once or twice as I stumbled in the darkness. But keeping track eased my mind from other dangers on this road. This was farther than I had ever been from my simple room behind the ovens. And still, the day had not yet yielded to the night. I have not yet escaped the spell hanging above the Lord's domain. I wonder if I ever will.

Along the way, I've passed others who fled before me. Some had fallen by the side of the road. A few found comfort at an abandoned inn at the crossroad, where they waited for the end. One desperate woman was trying to make it back. Sadly, in her weakened state, I knew she couldn't climb the hill.

Many are weak in Fioch Brae. The manor is dying along with the town and the lands on the plains below. Food is scarce, even for the baker's son. There's water in the wells, and the Dechtire River below the eastern bluff still has fish. But the farm animals are gone, having been slaughtered for either food or sacrifice. Hunters range farther and farther, seeking game.

But the Hunter above points the way. His constellation looms large in the dark, eastern sky, and the five stars of his spear point the way. That is the direction I follow.

Hours no longer have meaning, but I walked many of them. I can only judge by the soreness of my feet and the pain in my belly. When I arrived at the Old Stone Bridge, several others had already gathered. Some ventured to the crossing, peered over the edge, and drew back. Fear gripped them.

"What troubles you?" I asked.

One responded. "The mist over the river obscures the view of any figures on the far side. And legends say there's a troll or a changeling under this bridge that comes out when night arrives. Listen. You can hear it reveling in this endless night."

At that moment, the son of the baker became the leader of this band of wayfarers when, more determined than ever, I set foot on the bridge. Nothing rose from the space below to challenge me.

"I hear only the flow of water against the rocks beneath me."

I continued on. Halfway across, the mist and haze grew thick. I looked down to watch my footing. The world around me had turned black. With the next two steps, a sudden bright light blinded me before I was thrust back into darkness.

Closing my eyes, I inched forward. When I opened them again, there was a dim light. My shadow stretched out for ten feet in front of me! Startled, I stopped, but only for a moment. With the next two steps, my shadow shrank back to me. Heat fell on my face. I looked up to see the sun high above me. It was just below noon. Dusk was finally gone.

Behind me loomed a wall of darkness. Shadowy figures wavered beyond it.

"Come!" I screamed. "Come into the light. The day is warm and beautiful."

I ran down the other side of the stone bridge and dropped to my knees on the warm ground. I waited for the others to join me. Then I heard the sound of approaching hooves. When I raised my head, I saw a company of soldiers emerging from the wood, marching toward the bridge. They were ready for battle.

"Clear the road!" the leader ordered. He didn't slow down.

I quickly rolled aside into a patch of grass and wildflowers to avoid being trampled.

One of the last foot soldiers to pass extended a hand. "Keep moving. You aren't safe yet. A fortnight ago, the darkness hadn't yet reached the bridge. Soon it will be consumed. The Duke has declared that he will not allow it to overshadow Middle Wood." And then he was gone into the night.

Despite the weariness in my legs, I walked away unhurried. I still had eight hours of daylight left. I planned to enjoy them all. For me, it was a new day.

NEVERENDING

W HEN THE KLAXON SOUNDED, VALARON'S HEART LIFTED EVEN AS THE hair on his skin stood. Only one traveler had come down the bridge in the past century. Friend or foe, he flew with wings spread to their fullest to meet the returning soldier or invading enemy. Taking a position near the bridge's base, he drew his sword in salute.

Moments later, a reddish-black demon with three horns, tattered wings folded behind its back, and a bottle in its hand cantered down the ramp. His bare feet left a trail of dark, brimstone prints behind him that evaporated into rising smoke clouds.

Valaron lowered his sword, his face falling. "Oh, it's you, Rupsgath. Why have you returned?"

"I have come for you!" He raised the bottle high. "To get you drunk!"

"Why will you not leave me be? Be gone from Clarita, and return no more."

The demon sat heavily on a large stone. He sank his teeth into the bottle's cork and pulled it free with a satisfying pop. "Leave you be? It's been eighty years since I last came! Have you seen any other than me in all that time?"

Rupsgath tilted his head back, held the bottle above his maw, and poured himself a drink. Then he offered the bottle to his host. Valaron declined.

The demon shrugged and took a second swig. "You must realize by now that no one else is returning. The war is done. The combatants have all fallen...to their deaths or to some lower dimensions. Only you and I are left, guarding domains against non-existent invaders."

Valaron scoffed. "There are others out there. They didn't all go to war. Some traveled the planes. Scholars, emissaries! They'll return. And until they do, I will remain here. Someone must guard Clarita always, lest it become defiled!"

"The lone sentry. I know the job." He belched, emitting a wisp of smoke. "I handle that the way I deal with most things. Poorly. That's why I'm here."

"To torment me further?"

"No. To say 'Goodbye.' I've had enough of the solitary life, sitting on rocks in the middle of lava pools, just alone with my thoughts. And some booze."

He looked at the angel squarely. "I'm leaving. I'm going to walk the planes. Maybe I'll return in another hundred years, or maybe a thousand. Maybe not at all. But I'm finished watching over an empty domain, protecting it from outsiders. Like any creature in the heavens or hells would want to call it home!"

Putting the near-empty bottle down on the ground, Rupsgath stood and turned away. "You could come with me. Or we could go separate ways. But there's no one left to fight off." He left out a laugh. "If you stay, I believe the saying is that you can beat that sword into a plowshare."

Valaron raised his sword high again and shook his fist. "If you're determined to leave, then do so, and never darken the bridge again! I'll erect a fence around that defiled spot in your 'honor.'"

"As you desire." The demon walked the pavement to the bridge, his claws setting sparks on the stone. "If you ever do get tired of this place, visit Guumpthus. Take some holy water and sanctify a path. There'll be no infernal magic to counter it. Farewell."

The decrepit creature faded into the distance as the bridge crossed the planes.

Valaron thrust his sword into the dirt. Crops needed tending, and the steeple needed to be shined. He glanced back at the empty bridge once more. Maybe those would wait until tomorrow. Perhaps, he thought, I may take one day off.

THE DOG LISTENER

NEIGHBORHOODS CHANGE, AND MINE ISN'T ANY DIFFERENT. A FEW stores closed, and some boutiques and cafes replaced them. It's great if you need a hundred kinds of hot sauce.

Overall, I'd say that it's been a net positive since I like craft brews. But there wasn't anything wrong with how it was a couple of years ago. Plus, I miss the old guy at the newspaper shop. But rents get higher, and people retire.

The biggest change, if I had to pick one, is the local park. I work freelance. My apartment is my office. This allows me the flexibility to go out in the morning, and walk two blocks downtown to my favorite bench, overlooking my favorite patch of grass, between the fountain and the playground.

Physically, the park itself is the same. The people ambulating within its stone walls and iron gates? They're a different story.

Sure, some of the old-timers still show up to get their daily allotment of exercise and sunshine. Folks working nearby still stop in with bagged lunches on sunny days.

But where'd the kids go? Grown and moved on. Families have left the cramped apartments of these old wood-framed houses for bigger spaces. These days, I could sit on a swing for an hour, lost in my thoughts, and it wouldn't bother anyone. There's no one to bother.

The younger crowd that's moved in aren't interested in begetting progeny just yet. What do they want instead? Dogs.

Why not? They're man's best friend, right? Even mine, until I turned thirteen, and found out I was allergic to Prince, my family's Doberman Shepherd mutt.

Now that, by itself, isn't enough for me to alter my daily constitutionals. Yes, maybe it's turning into a dog park, but there's still plenty of fresh air. I can keep my distance from the fur and dander. And, to be fair, the owners clean up after their companions better than some parents ever did with their kids.

No, what bothers me is that the sounds of children's laughter and their shrieks of joy have been replaced with a constant barrage of "Fetch!" and "Who's a good boy?" Not the guy in the oversized college football jersey, fake-throwing the tennis ball for the fifth time! He's not a good boy.

Plus, there's one more little thing, which I'm hesitant to mention. You'll think I'm lying or just plain nuts.

I can hear dogs' thoughts. I *understand* their thoughts.

How this happened, I can't begin to say I know for sure. Last fall, I was in a car accident, bumped my head, had an MRI. Got tested for neurological issues—nothing found. Even had a bad case of food poisoning along the way that left me as sick as a...well, really sick for a week.

But since then, I hear their thoughts, such as they are. And they aren't deep.

"Fetch the ball. Fetch the ball. Where's the ball? He still has the ball. He threw the ball. There's the ball. There it is. Bring it back. Bring back the ball. He threw the ball. Fetch ..."

"Rub my belly. Rub my belly. Rub my belly..."

"I'm a good dog! I'm a good dog! I'm a good dog!"

Their conversational choices are limited, and I can't even speak to them. Believe me, I tried. They don't understand me. They just tilt their heads and stare, like I'm the odd one. Maybe I am.

Then today I spot some large, black breed of wolfhound. It was huge and alone. Did it get loose? Did someone think it was a good idea to let a creature that size roam free? I wasn't getting near it to check for a collar or tags.

Thank God, there weren't any children about to frighten. That thing creeped the bejeezus out of *me*. My allergies kicked in just looking its direction. If it decided to pad my way, I'd need more than a box of Kleenex — I'd need a new pair of boxers!

It plodded over to the milestone marker, a four-foot-tall obelisk in the center of the park. It stood on its hind legs, resting its front paws as if it were a podium. From there, it surveyed the crowd.

I hadn't heard it utter a sound. I assumed that was because I was too far away, or maybe because fear had overtaken my brain. But then I heard a low, gravelly...*demonic* voice. "Fetch the soul! Fetch the soul! Fetch the soul!!"

It turned in my direction, gazed right at me...right through me. "Have you seen the soul?"

I selected "flight" from the psychological checklist, but this devil dog was in front of me before I could move. It closed the gap to my bench, taking only three strides. Then this cursed canine rested a paw on either side of me. With its face just inches from mine, fiery-red eyes stared through the windows of my soul. Brimstone exuded from its nostrils. Acidic drool dripped onto my lap, burning holes in my jeans.

"I have to fetch the soul. Have you seen the soul?" I heard its thoughts, and I knew it could hear mine. I could feel it inside my head.

A wave of images flashed across my mind. Snippets of everyone I'd seen today. One lingered a second longer than the rest, a muscle-bound guy with a crew cut. He wore a tank top and took in the Vitamin D, unconcerned about the possibility of melanomas.

The Beast pivoted its enormous snout nearly a full 180 degrees. Behind it, on the far side of the park, I caught sight of the guy from the vision. As if he felt our combined stares, he turned toward us. Horrified, he broke into an all-out sprint for the wall and scrambled up.

The hound took off like a bat out of...well, you know. Galloping at a speed that would shame a Derby champion, it hurdled the high stone wall like it was a little red wagon. Maybe it was just an afterimage burned into my tearing eyes, but I could swear I saw a trail of black smoke as the ungodly creature disappeared from view. I shut my eyes and caught my breath.

Oddly, no one else in the park seemed to have noticed any of what had just taken place. Less odd, many were now staring at me. They clearly wondered if I was going to clean up after myself and the mess I'd just made.

It got me to thinking. Maybe it was time to find a new place to go to meditate on my life. After all, the neighborhood has seriously changed recently.

LAST DAWN

A LONE FIGURE STOOD NEAR THE EDGE OF THE CLIFF, SILHOUETTED BY the full moon. "Count" Andrew Sumner listened as the waves crashed into the rocky shore below. He wore his best suit, with his vintage opera cape closed against the wind. Someone of his advanced years needed protection from the elements. Then he laughed at that thought and tossed his cape into the air. It flapped and fluttered in the breeze, landing behind him somewhere. He stretched his arms wide to take in the beautiful night. One final night.

The ocean nearly drowned the sound of footsteps on gravel. He turned to spy his servant take a position a few feet behind him. "Look at it, George. The night we picked turned out better than we could have dreamed. If I still had dreams. It's been a long time. It's the one thing I miss about this existence. And yet, I am still reluctant to see it end. But it must, I know. All things must end."

He stared at the tumult of the water below and smiled. "I look forward to seeing the dawn."

George nodded, standing silent. He looked past Sumner to the light of the moon on the waves.

"Indulge me, George. The last time I saw a sunrise was a cold morning in St. Albans. That's just north of London. Little did I know what that next night would bring, and how it would change me.

"And look at the water. When did I last see the sun rise over water? I can't remember. Perhaps as a boy in Ipswich. Ironic, George, when you consider I spent two months crossing the Atlantic. That's how long it took back then!"

Sumner turned away from the edge. Headlights approached, momentarily blinding him. The car's brakes squealed as it pulled over. A door slammed shut, and someone ran toward them. In the moonlight, Sumner could make out the figure of a young woman approaching. George held up a hand to her, and she stopped in her tracks.

"No, George," Sumner said, smiling, "allow her to come closer. I'm happy you've invited your lady friend. I fear you may need her when morning comes. The separation could be painful."

The Count took only a step in her direction. The woman breathed heavily, her heart pounding in her chest, eyes wide with both fear and concern. He'd seen her before. She was a lovely young thing. He was about to bow in salutation when he spotted his cape on the ground. Picking it up, he shook it once in the wind before donning it again with a flourish. Now he could welcome her with a grand, regal gesture.

"Miss, in this short time we have, may I regale you with the story of how I came to Maine? It was in the years after the Revolution. Oh, that was a great time to be alive! And I *was* alive, in my own way. No, war is a terrible thing, but this was a war for a cause, and I fought as bravely as the soldiers I fed upon. I never wanted in the evenings, my hunger easily sated."

Sumner entertained the pair, as the hours passed, with tales of colonial life. How he started a business for financial security, with the aid of servants like George. How he finally stopped wandering and put down roots. He spoke of the many people he'd encountered, some of whom made their way into history books, while these stories he told did not. So engaged were they with reminiscing, the three almost made no note of the lightening sky.

It was George who interrupted. He pointed to the east. "Count Sumner, look!"

Sumner turned to face the end of this life. Would there still be anything after? Or was any such chance irrevocably lost in the past? Either way, he'd grown weary of this life. It was time.

Eager anticipation mixed with terror as he steeled himself for the coming of this new day. As the minutes passed, the sun rose slowly out of the Atlantic, shining its rays onto the Maine coastline and the three figures on the clifftop.

"It's beautiful." Sumner smiled and stared directly into its light. This was it. Soon it would be over. He'd be free of this life.

He felt the warmth on his face, something he hadn't felt on his skin in so long. Peacefulness. Serenity.

But it fled in an instant, as Sumner thrust his hands up to shield his shut eyes. Pain consumed him. He dropped to his knees, screaming into the morning sky. His mind raced through centuries of memories, searching for peaceful moments, only to have each devoured by the torment. It felt like fire enveloped him.

Falling forward, he grabbed his chest, gasping for air. Then he realized the screams were not his own. He opened his eyes and looked down at his hand on the cool grass, unblemished, unsinged. He fell backward and turned toward the others.

The woman had moved away, mouth agape, watching in horror as smoke and flames engulfed George, who had also collapsed to the ground. George smiled at Sumner through the pain.

"You have served me well, Andrew. Thank you. For your many years of loyalty, I have left everything in your name. The estate. The business. All of it is yours now. You tell my stories well. Please, remember them."

George looked to the woman with his final words. "Take care of him, my dear. He'll need you."

With a final scream, George fell, consumed by fire, until only charred fabric and ash remained.

The woman ran to Andrew, knelt beside him, and wrapped him in her arms. An embrace for the ages. "Grandpa," she whispered. "It's Alice. You're free now."

Looking up to the sun again, Sumner felt the warmth of the morning, as well as the warmth of his granddaughter's hug. Memories stirred within, and for the first time in a long time, Sumner felt alive.

HELL'S DINER

DAMON OXHORN WORKED THE COUNTER AT THE SIN CAFE AS HE'D done for countless aeons. Most days, he put in double shifts, which not only seemed to last forever but quite possibly did. An eternity could pass before relief came, but that was sort of the point of damnation. So day-in, day-out, eternity-in, eternity-out, he stood on his cloven hooves with a fresh dish-towel, wiping down the counter.

A blood-curdling scream accompanied the opening of the diner's front door, as an infernal tether choked a condemned soul trapped in a cubbyhole just above the head jamb. A short, stocky, and hairy demon entered, its furry wings tucked behind it. It scanned the near-empty establishment and shuffled its knobby, taloned feet to its usual booth in the corner.

When no one appeared to take its order, Damon hollered out a curse. The satyress, a copper-skinned beauty from the waist up, answered the summons. Deomica, Waitress of the Dark, gave Damon a look that would kill a mortal. She bit her fangs into her lower lip to avoid talking back to the boss. But that didn't stop her from shaking her goat rump and stubby tail in his direction as she took out her order pad.

None of this bothered Damon. He took his job seriously as part-owner of the diner, even suggested calling it a "café" to class the place up a bit. This was mostly lost on the clientele. If his regular customers appreciated anything, it was that Damon made sure everything was served piping hot, including the root beer.

He watched as Deomica exchanged some fiery words with the customer. Those two tormented each other on a regular basis.

After a few minutes of foreplay, she cantered up to the kitchen window and hollered in. "Adam and Eve on a raft—Toss 'em out of Paradise!"

Scant feet away, a spatula landed with a heavy thud. A gravelly voice bellowed out, "It's 'wreck 'em!'. Get it right! Adam and Eve on a raft—wreck 'em. You sorry excuse for a succubus!"

"Bite your forked tongue!" she snapped back. Looking down, she brushed her hand across the matted fur on her left hip and thigh. "True, I do have the legs for that line of work."

She turned back to Damon. "Where did you find him anyway? It's enough to make me hang up my smock!"

"No!" Damon chortled. "All you're wearing is that smock. This ain't that kind of establishment!"

After hanging the ticket in the rack, she grabbed the coffee pot and trotted back to the table.

Coffee was Damon's specialty. His Lava Java blend could literally melt your tongue. That kind of thing happened a lot if you didn't take the necessary precautions. Not that such an injury couldn't be mended. More likely, it just wouldn't be.

When she went back to the table with the mug, Damon heard an exasperated grunt from the kitchen behind him. "That woman!"

Damon's employee-of-the-month slaved over the open fire pit in the next room, thanks to a combination of mutual agreement and a little eternal damnation. Devlin Pigsnout had porcine complexion topped by a single twisted horn. For the past century, he'd manned the grill, but he was no short-order cook. A short cook, certainly, with a barreled chest, hairy forelimbs, and tattered batlike wings rarely seen in this region of the Abyss. He was also a short-tempered cook, without a doubt.

But short-order cook? Feh! Devlin worked his demonic magic in the blackened culinary arts like no other. He took great pride in his work. And greed, too. And lust. Pretty much all of the top Deadly Sins, except sloth.

There was nothing slow about his work, his passion. He could move quite quickly and dexterously, with even a certain degree of stealth, despite the large, ominous chains that bound him. And though he had eternity at his fingertips, he spared not one picosecond when completing his creations. No matter the task set before him, he could whip up a masterpiece and beat it into shape in short order.

Okay, so maybe he was a "short order" cook, but only in that sense of the term.

Damon Oxhorn admired the heated fervor Devlin poured into his platters. In fact, he thought the chef over-committed himself, given a clientele unlikely to be appreciative of his devotions.

When the waitress returned to the counter, she confronted the cook. "Hey, Pigsnout! I have to ask. With all the diners in all the circles of Hell, how did you fall into this one? I've trolled these brimstone pits for half a millennium now. And in all that time, I've never seen a creature like you. What's your story?"

Damon hadn't thought about it before, but he didn't know the answer either. It hadn't crossed his mind until now. He and Deomica stood and stared into the deep, dark, dank hole that was the kitchen. Silence dragged on as the seconds ticked away like sand falling through a three-minute timer. And when the last grain fell, a hairy paw reached through the window and deposited a platter with two perfectly scrambled eggs on medium toast, with a side of damnation hellfries and appropriate garnish. Presentation was everything.

"Order up!" the husky voice croaked. "Then I'll tell you the story."

Deomica hurdled a chair and swiftly deposited the hot plate in front of the hellion, who barely looked up from his newspaper. She returned at full gallop to the counter like it was the home stretch at Belmont. "Okay, spill."

Devlin looked up at his boss, who nodded back to him.

"You know how they say that poison is a women's weapon? It's also the perfect cover for a man."

Deomica interrupted. "Wait! You were a man? A human man? How long ago was that? What happened to you?"

A low growl built up, and he barked out an answer. "That's what I'm telling you! Four hundred years ago, I was known from Naples to Bari. I opened a shop, and a line formed outside my doors. Fathers wanted me to teach their sons. Mothers wanted me to marry their daughters. Well, I did teach the boys a few things, but I only met halfway on the marriage offers.

"Who needed one young wife anyway, when there were scores of older wives in loveless, arranged marriages? Few noticed the ladies coming around my kitchen door, begging for scraps. But I noticed many were fairly-dressed and pleasantly plump. Were they starving? Yes, they were starving, alright! And they were sated, if you know what I mean."

Rolling eyes and gagging sounds indicated Deomica knew. "So you banged a bunch of old moglies. And...?"

"They start telling me dreams, if they were free. And how grateful they might be. Appreciative. Next thing, they bring their husbands around for seven-course dinners, with some added ingredients in the struffoli! A few drops of aqua tofana in their espresso. She came into his money, and I came into her bed. Until the next lady came round, or until I had to pack up and leave town."

"Leave? Why would you leave? You had a sweet deal going."

"Too sweet. And I didn't want my tea sweetened! Why do you think I was known from Naples to Bari? They didn't have telephones then! But after a hundred lovely widows or so, it was two cugine who did me in. One was sleeping with the other's husband, and she wasn't happy he was gone. Because now she had to go back to her own husband, the cornuto. She's the one who put the horns on me, figuratively speaking. Pretty much literally, too, as it turned out."

Deomica looked him over and shrugged. "Okay, say I believe you. That was 400 years ago. There are 300 years missing."

He laughed, belching up some brimstone. "You ever hear of Azragrog the Unstoppable?"

Damon chuckled. "A devil powerful enough to be nearly a demigod in his own right. I haven't heard much about him lately, though. What about him?"

Devlin put his paws on the counter and started brushing out tics. "I'd been burning in some molten pit for over a century when he pulled me out of that vile muck. He'd heard my story, and wanted me to work for him. And I did for two centuries. Until one day, I poisoned his entire court. He was no longer Unstoppable. As punishment, I was cast down here."

Damon looked deep into his cook's eye, searching for what was left of his soul. "Forget how for a moment. Why? Why would you poison his entire court?"

Deomica laughed. "Isn't it obvious? They insulted his cooking."

With an orcish grin, Devlin picked up his spatula and returned to his grill. Damon glanced at the corner booth to see if his patron was enjoying his breakfast. Looking around the near-empty diner, he wondered if any of his old regulars had insulted his cook recently.

THE THING ABOUT HUMANS

THE THING ABOUT HUMANS…" THE OLD GRAY CAT BEGAN HIS STORY, TO the delight of the kittens seated around him. Then he licked the back of his left front paw and rubbed a spot behind his ear.

A little black-and-orange-striped tom jumped up, edging forward. "What's the thing? What's the thing?"

Grizabella had been resting by the fire, just behind the littlest ones. She stepped into the circle, lifted the kitten by the scruff of the neck, and put him back in his place. "Settle down, Rum Tum." She nodded to Old Deuteronomy, then returned to her spot, circled three times, and reclined next to little Skimbleshanks.

Old Deuteronomy rested his chin on his paws and continued his story.

"The thing about humans is that they had three different names. Sounds mad, does it not? But it was true. First was the name that the world would know them by. They had a family name, which was the name of their clan or their pride. Something like Smith or Jones or Black or Green. And they had a given name, which is where it gets funny. You see, the given name is the name the family would call them. And a human cub would be given both these names!"

The kittens rolled around, laughing at this silliness. Victoria bumped into Electra, and the two started wrestling until Grizabella hissed, then they started snuggling together instead.

Old Deuteronomy coughed and continued. "The second was their fancy name, like Crazy Joe or Sally-Boy or Brainiac or Nicky Tree Fingers. Names used by their closest friends in the other clans."

The little calico, Plato, lost interest in the tale when he spied a spot of light before him and readied himself to pounce. Old Deuteronomy reached out a paw and smacked Mistoffelees on the back of the head. The all-black kitten yowled, and the conjured light disappeared, to Plato's disappointment.

"However," Old Deuteronomy continued. "They had a third name, a unique name. This was the name that only the human knew. This was the name for how they saw themselves. What they desired. What they strived for. Some of them searched their whole lives to discover what this name was. Some never found out."

Rum Tum sat up on his hind legs and swat at a mote of dust, illuminated by the fire behind him. "They didn't know their own names?"

The old cat shook his head from side to side. "No, little one. Many never discovered their true calling. Imagine a tabby going through the motions of hunting mice but never knowing why they hunted."

Rum Tum's eyes grew wide, and he tilted his head sideways until he almost turned over. "I don't get it."

Old Deuteronomy ruffled the fur on the top Rum Tum's head and smiled. "You will, my boy. One day."

Mistoffelees rolled onto his back, cackling and punching the air. "What a silly story! And you're falling for it!"

"Am not!" Rum Tum shot back. "Besides, it's true. Old Deuteronomy doesn't make up his tales!"

In an instant, the black cat flipped over again, sitting on his haunches. "If it's true, then where are these humans now? What happened to them? Humans are as real as fairies or ogres or elemaphants!"

"They're gone. They left us." Grizabella barely looked up, stroking young Morgan's matted fur. "They had their day in the Sun, and they moved on."

Old Deuteronomy rose and circled about little Mistoffelees, who spun around, not wanting the old cat to get behind him. "Some say they went up into the sky to find a new world. Some say they went down into the dirt and were no more. But up or down, they once were here." He sat back and searched the night sky. "Wherever they are, if they still are, they've gone from this place. It's ours now."

An ember popped in the fire, sending up a geyser of sparks. The little cats jumped and ran to watch the show, chasing down every twinkle and flicker. Storytime was forgotten.

Old Deuteronomy padded his way beside Grizabella. "Ours now," she repeated, nuzzling under the older cat's chin. "And it will be theirs when, like the humans, we're just memories."

ONCE UPON A TIME...

S ITTING ON MY DECK, A QUIET, PRIVATE BEACH STRETCHED OUT BEFORE
me. I relaxed in a lounge chair with the sun shining down on
my legs. I wore a short cotton tank dress. I had a magazine in one
hand and a glass of white wine in the other—nothing out of the
ordinary. But when I looked up to watch the waves roll in with
the high tide, that's when a curious thing occurred.

As the late afternoon sun shone down, reflecting off the water,
a figure started to rise up from beneath the waves. I blinked
twice, believing it a trick of reflected light, but she was still out
there in deep water, where no one had been before. Thinking she
was in trouble, I jumped up and ran to the shore, crossing the
hot sand in my bare feet.

By the time I reached the water's edge, she had already
emerged, except...except she had brought a piece of the ocean
with her. This strange woman stood on the shore before me. A
wreath of coral adorned her long orange-and-red-streaked hair.
She wore a gown made of waves, crashing and breaking all about
her, with a train that stretched far back into the sea behind her.
The susurrus of the waves sounded in every step she took, and
I felt a cool spray brush my skin as she approached. Glistening
in the sunlight, the swirling seafoam did little to hide the beauty
of the creature beneath.

Where had she come from? Had she emerged from the ocean
or out of a fairy tale?

She seemed unsteady on her feet. Instinctively, I reached out
to her. When she took my hand, the ebb and flow of her sleeve
enveloped my arm. I watched as it ran up and back past my
elbow. Then I looked up at her in wonderment. Her skin was a

pale shade of blue, and her eyes, a deep sapphire that I could get lost in. I offered a smile, and she returned it. Then we each reached out for the other with our free hands.

The moment we touched, my heart leapt with excitement even as a surge crashed upon the beach, showering us. My dress, drenched and clinging to my body, now revealed as much as her living gown. We laughed for a moment. Then she slowly pulled our hands to her side, drawing me in closer. I closed my eyes, and our lips met.

She led me a few steps closer to the water before I pulled her a few steps up the sand. She glanced back at her crystal-clear, sparkling train, stretched thin to the rolling waves.

"I can't go any farther," she said. "I'll die."

"But I'll drown if I go with you."

"I can protect you."

"How?"

Throwing her arms around me, she reeled me in and kissed me again. Longer. Deeper. Her salty lips parted, and I felt the breath of the ocean. It consumed me, clouding my mind, but I felt so happy, so alive. I heard a choir of heavenly voices singing my bliss.

When that moment of euphoria faded, I realized that she'd led me knee-deep into the surf. Shocked to my senses, I let go of her arms and jumped back, retreating to the beach.

Surprised and saddened, she looked at me as she receded farther out, sinking down to her waist. Her eyes lost a little of their sparkle. I couldn't tell if I had splashed her face, or if I saw a tear.

As I watched her descend into the undulating swells, I couldn't deny my feelings, my longing.

"Wait!" I screamed and ran back into the ocean.

Her smile glittered over her entire face, and mine, as well, like sunlight on the ocean. She waved her arm deliberately in the water. A ripple headed toward me. It quickly swelled until it washed over me, knocking me from my feet. Submerged, I struggled to hold what breath I had as I felt the pull of the undertow dragging me out to sea. In desperation, I clawed at the sand until I made it up to dry land once more, coughing and gasping for air.

As I caught my breath, I realized what had happened, what I'd done. I rolled over and looked out to sea. It was too late, though. The last strands of her coral-adorned hair sank beneath the waves. The sun quickly followed. I don't know how long I sat, staring out over the ocean. Darkness consumed everything, including me. She was gone...and I didn't even know her name.

I've come back every sunset for the past three years. I sit on the beach and think about that intriguing woman I met...once upon a time. I wonder who she was and where she lived beneath the waves. Were there cities or kingdoms like in the fairy tales? Would they be wondrous to behold?

I wanted the answers. I yearned for those answers. My heart still swelled with the current. And I waited, and watched, and hoped that someday I would find those answers...find her. But that's the sad truth of fairy tales. Once upon a time only happens once.

REALISM

THE IT GIRL

THE GRAYNESS OF MY MOOD MATCHED THE SWIRLING MAELSTROM OF finger paint before me. Other kids had taken all the colors and left me in a world of black and white. The morning brightened a little when the blonde offered to share the blue and yellow. She was the kind of babe who put the "kinder" in kindergarten. I was in the home stretch to be sharing juice boxes by snack time when trouble approached in a green shirt and jeans, interrupting playtime.

Red-headed and freckle-faced, I knew she'd been around the blocks a bit. Nearly an inch taller than me, she cast an imposing shadow in the light of the overhead fluorescents. But I had on my Big Boy pants, and I thought I was ready for anything. Little did I know...

Her coy smile concealed her devilish interior underneath a welcoming, colorful wrapper. I was entranced when I should have been wary. So I didn't suspect anything when she reached out a hand, her fingers stained red from an unfortunate incident with the washable Crayolas. Her touch was electric with the static energy from the Reading Time rug.

"Tag," she whispered. "You're It!"

Red turned and ran as soon as she delivered the bad news. I turned to Blondie and watched her recoil in fear. She yanked off her smock, revealing a Dora top beneath, then scurried off like an explorer without a map.

Like the proverbial cheese, I stood alone. I had painted myself into a corner. But I was still crafty. Just past a couple of Jills playing jacks, I spied a bad hat climbing on bookcases. He was trying to reach to the top stories and was about to take a fall.

Sure, I thought, *I may be It, but as long as no one tattles to Miss Cyndi, I won't be It by naptime.*

BLOCK

T HERE HAD BEEN FOUR DEATHS ALREADY, AND A FIFTH WAS COMING soon. *It's too many*, Josh thought. *Too quickly. But what can I do about it?*

There was an old saw he used and trusted: "kill someone every twenty pages to keep it interesting." But, so far, he had only written sixty pages. Where was it going? Could he kill the former roommate so soon? Or should it be the cheating girlfriend?

He was stuck. Again.

There were so many paths to choose from going forward. *Why can't I decide?* he thought. The doubt unsettled him.

Black letters on a white page against a blue background taunted him. Josh lifted an arm from the keyboard to shut off the monitor but pulled back. Instead, he swiveled about and abandoned that seat, plopping down in the armchair next to his desk.

The room was dark except for the quivering flames of a dozen scented candles scattered around to set the mood. The glow of the monitor beside him also illuminated the smoky haze. Josh reached for the TV remote but realized that would kill the vibe, break his concentration. He needed to think, so he lit a joint off one of the candles. That would help him relax.

Josh kept to a daily routine. He thought it invigorating. Just as often, he found it infuriating. *Do the actions of the past shape the future? Are people bound by their past actions? Can someone move past them, or do they drive their story, the unwritten narrative yet to unfold?*

So lost in his meditations, Josh didn't hear the doorbell ring. It wasn't until the pounding began that he came back into his own mind. Sluggishly, he rose and crossed the room.

He opened the basement door to find his girlfriend April standing on the second of the six steps leading up to his mom's backyard. Rain fell behind her, running down the stairs to the drain below.

Like a beautiful rose, he thought, *blooming in May showers.* Josh looked into her eyes, as radiant as star sapphires or lapis lazuli! *Has she returned to me?*

He stared at her until she broke the silence.

"Can I come in, Josh? I'm getting wet out here."

He stepped aside and bid her enter.

"Why is it so dark in here?"

She reached for the light switch, but Josh caught her hand. It felt good to hold it again. "I like it this way. It helps me write."

April left out an exasperated groan and pulled her hand free. "Ugh! Writing! Always the writing! Josh, listen to me. You've been 'writing' for three years now. But you haven't written anything!"

Not true! He had sixty pages! And at least a dozen short stories almost finished, plus outlines for six more novels once he got the first one done. But this one had to be great, or he'd never get the chance to write the other six.

"Josh, you need to give this up."

"What? Why?"

"You're living in your mother's basement, for God's sake! You need to get a real job that pays real dollars. You can't pay the bills with 'contributor copies'! You need a regular paycheck to cover the rent."

The rent! That was it. He knew who had sent her and what he wanted.

He tried not to sneer when he spoke. "So, how is Randall doing?"

April felt her way around the dimly lit room looking for someplace to sit. "He was fine, last I saw him. He still needs a roommate. And he'll get one sooner or later."

Josh closed and bolted the door and returned to his arm-chair. "I wish him luck with that."

She sighed. "He would take you back in a minute if you just got a real job. He's even willing to give you time to repay what you owe him."

Josh stared at the shadows dancing on his girlfriend's face. "So, you've talked with him recently?"

"Well…" April looked away, as if hiding her expression in the darkness. "Okay, yes, I've been by the apartment a few times. But only because we've been talking about you. We want to help you, Josh. You have friends!"

Friends can make you a better person, he thought. *They can make you the best version of you there is if you let them.* But he wondered as he took another drag, *Do these "friends" really know me? Could they really make me better if they didn't?*

And then a lucid thought came to him. "'Friends'? Just 'friends'?"

"Josh!" April protested.

He thought he heard tears in her voice.

He put the joint down. "I thought maybe you came because you wanted to get together. Maybe stay a while."

"Seriously? Here? In your *mother's* basement? Do you listen to yourself? We're not sixteen anymore, Josh."

And there it was. He snuffed out his smoke and stared at the stained shag carpet. What were the paths moving forward? He shuffled his feet, thinking about it.

"I'm sorry, Josh. Now…now isn't a good time for that. I'm, uh…"

"…with Randall?"

It was her turn to look at the floor, but only for a moment. And that had been enough. "Can we please turn on the lights? I can't even see your face with the glare from the monitor."

"It'll break the mood."

"There's! No! Mood! And what kind of candles are these? There's a funky smell."

"Are sure it isn't—"

"It's not the pot!"

She leaped up to turn on the lights. Josh jumped after her, but stumbled on some discarded refuse, knocking over a candle.

It landed on a pile of dirty T-shirts, which promptly caught fire. So consumed with snuffing out the flames, he didn't realize that the lights had come on until he heard her loud gasp.

He looked up but had to shield his eyes from the brightness of the flickering fluorescent bulbs. April had her hands over her mouth and nose.

This man cave was not fit for living in. The floor was covered with discarded take-out, used plates, and napkins. Dirty laundry lay scattered about the room.

When April had caught her breath, she lowered her hands and tried to speak. "How, Josh? How did it get this bad in just a few weeks?"

Then something else caught her eye. Toward the front of the house, past the idle washer and dryer, a lumpy tarp lay on the floor between a workbench and the furnace. If nothing else, it was a worse fire hazard than all the candles.

April navigated the minefield before her. Josh tried to stop her, failing once again. She yanked the tarp away and froze in horror. The tile floor had been shattered, and the earth beneath removed to make room for a body, which was not completely buried. She wanted to scream, but dropped to her knees and wretched instead.

Josh walked up behind her slowly. He grabbed a two-by-four from the workbench. She turned and looked up at him.

She whimpered, "Josh, no..."

Their eyes met, and neither one held back their tears. It lasted but a moment before Josh had to look away. *So many paths to choose...*

"Josh, please," she begged. "I—I can help."

He tried to listen to himself, but April was still pleading.

"We can get you the help you need. It will be all right."

Right? Write! He still had more to write. And he wouldn't... *couldn't* give that up.

He looked down one more time at his girlfriend. His former girlfriend. His cheating girlfriend. Tears ran down her face like...*like the rain off a beautiful, blooming rose in May.* But the sparkle had left her eyes. They both knew how the story had begun and how it would end. The actions of the past shape the future.

He threw the tarp over her so he wouldn't have to watch when he brought down the block of wood.

When it was over, Josh looked around, trying to take in everything that had happened. Feel it. Experience it for a second time. There were plenty of things that had to be taken care of now. But first, he sat back down in the swivel chair in front of his computer. Once more, he stared at the screen. There had been five murders, but he knew what path to choose. At least, for the next twenty pages....

NUMBER 17
BRIAR ROSE LANE

As much as I like to be unpredictable, I do enjoy keeping to a routine. So while I rise each morning with the Sun, I vary the time I first look out the window, or when I take my morning constitutional down to the shops on Lavender Road. I enjoy the food at the café, even if the morning paper is just a collection of misinformation. At least the rugby and football scores are true.

Despite the irregularity of my morning routine, when I departed my villa today at 9:01 a.m., the occupant of Number 24 Yarrow Way was waiting on the Village Green. I don't know his name, nor does he know mine. We've never inquired, and if either were to offer that information, the other would be reluctant to accept it. Oddly, today he had a companion, a younger man, and that piqued my interest.

Number 24 glanced down at his watch when he saw me approaching. He held out his left arm toward me and tapped the crystal. "*Vous êtes dehors tôt aujourd'hui.*" He tends to greet me in French, German, Russian, and other tongues, just to test me, expecting me to "slip up." While most of the residents stick to English, some tend to surprise you, like the Asian woman who speaks Welsh like a native or the Middle Eastern man who primarily converses in Polish. What else they know is anyone's guess.

When I simply raised an eyebrow in response, he turned an arm to the other gentleman. "Have you met my new neighbor, Number 87?" He then told the newcomer, "This is the fellow from 17 Briar Rose Lane."

"Neighbor?" I asked.

Number 24 laughed. "Yes, they finally renovated those bungalows on Primrose Path, and Number 87 lies just beyond my back yard. We met as he was crossing through to get to the main road."

Looking at the three of us, only one didn't have gray hair, and that one possibly still had his baby teeth. "You're a resident? I assumed you worked here. A little young to be in our retirement community, aren't you?"

"Probably." A pained smile disappeared quickly. "But I may not be here too long. I'm told this village would be a pleasant way to spend my days."

I shrugged. "I can't disagree so long as you take some precautions."

"Precautions?"

"Mostly the things you say and share. When your basic needs are taken care of, and other necessities are paid for, information becomes the greatest currency. Be careful when answering questions. Everyone is looking for information."

Number 24 clapped his hand on 87's shoulder. "Didn't I tell you 17 knows how things work?"

Ignoring my friendly adversary, I addressed the young man. "May I assume you left the game because of a medical condition?"

He started to answer and then reconsidered. "You…may assume that. Or anything else you'd like." A proper response. He was already learning.

We were interrupted by a call from the other side of the green. We turned to see a lovely, silver-haired vixen in a yellow sundress and a wide-brimmed straw hat waving in our direction. "Hello!" she called again.

The young lad seemed confused, but Number 24 took note. "Isn't that the lady from your street? Anything we should know?"

"Should?" I asked. "If we kissed, I wouldn't tell. But I did enjoy some wonderful pasta at Number 14 Briar Rose last week."

The woman seemed to glide effortlessly across the green to greet me. I took her offered hand and gave a slight bow.

"I didn't see you at the café this morning," she said. "You worried me terribly."

"Sorry to keep you waiting. We were welcoming our new resident here."

She glanced past me, looking our new arrival up and down. Twice. At least. Like an old cat still on the prowl. "Well, look at this young bud! Did someone plant an annual here among the perennials?"

Without another word, she released my hand. Then she slid past me and slipped her arm around his. "Well, now, as I have recently been stood up for breakfast, you will just have to join me for coffee and biscuits. Tell me all about how you came to choose this place."

87 barely gave protest as 14 led him away. It was all I could do to suppress my mirth.

"Perhaps I'll visit the barber first, and visit the café later for lunch. Just to change up the routine."

This shocked 24 more visibly than he usually allowed. "*Je verandert nooit je routine.*"

We watched the pair recede with 14 laughing gaily and patting 87's arm. I told 24, "We'll need to keep an eye on him."

"*On ne pervvy molodoy chelovek, kotorogo oni poslahi syuda, chtoby shpionit' za name.*"

No, I thought. And he won't be the last young man they send to spy on us, either.

CAPTAIN UNCLE

T HE CAPTAIN STUDIED THE MAP IN HIS QUARTERS AS THE SLOOP ROCKED gently in the warm waters off the Spanish Main. In the back corner, a young lad of barely a dozen years sat at the writing desk, surrounded by books. Captain Edward Coyle turned to leave when the boy called out, "Uncle!"

Coyle looked back and glared.

"I mean, 'Captain.' Uncle. Sir."

He nodded. "What now, William?"

The boy closed his book with a finger holding the page, smiling mischievously. "Why are goats popular with pirates all across the seas?"

Not a serious question, the Captain could tell. He didn't venture a response though he knew what his men would say after a few fingers of rum. And also what some might actually do with a goat after a skinful, given their less-than-reputable companions at their last port.

He allowed the barest hint of a smile. "You're the one with the studies, lad. You tell me."

"Because," William grinned, "in Tortuga, they can sell goats for a 'buck an ear,' but in Algiers, they buy 'em for their 'coarse hairs'!"

Crossing to the desk, he took the book from the boy and flipped through its pages. "Lad, you worry about your studies and let the crew worry about the goats." He put the book back on the desk. "You need to learn your letters. Since the carpenter drowned, there are only two men on board who can read. Me, and Parker, who writes and keeps the Articles of Conduct. I need you to read—and write—all the words if you're going to find a place on this ship."

Coyle pushed the book back to William and walked to the door. He straightened his vest, with its four flintlock pistols, then adjusted his belt with a dirk and a cutlass hanging on either side. He paused before leaving. "William, are you aware just what separates you from the rest of those sea dogs out there?"

William nodded. "Blood. We're kin."

Being the Captain's nephew, William had the run of the ship and could go almost anywhere he wanted. But being a cabin boy, he had duties of his own, running errands for the crew. And he'd better be quick about it. The men wouldn't taunt or tease him because of his blood. But they had the Captain's permission to discipline him—nay, not just permission, but orders to—should he ever be found slacking. William remembered his place and treated every last scamp and scalawag with respect.

"Aye, that's true. The blood of my beloved sister, God rest her soul, runs through your veins. But that's not the only way that blood sets you apart from them."

The boy raised an eyebrow, curious, but remained silent.

"Stay here and think on it a while," his uncle said. "We'll talk more later, after we relieve a Spanish trader of a little silver or some jewels." He stopped in the doorway and let out a belly laugh that could have filled the sails. "Who knows? Maybe we'll find a few goats!"

Then just as suddenly, he stopped laughing. "Stay in the cabin."

And with that, he left the boy alone.

Several hours had passed when the captain burst through the door, buoyed by Roberts, the coxswain, who helped Coyle to his cot. William leapt up to help as Third-mate Marlott, the ship's surgeon, followed with the medical bag.

Marlott held up a hand. "Keep back, lad. Give me room." The surgeon checked the injury in Captain Coyle's lower left side. "Luck is with you. The ball went straight through." He handed a bottle of whiskey to the captain, who took a swig and passed it back. Then Marlott poured the alcohol on the wound. The captain emitted a loud growl as the doctor wrapped the injury.

William watched patiently until he could wait no more. "What happened?"

Coyle laughed, which caused him to wince at the sudden pain. "Aye, it was a good day! Except for the part where a Spanish cur pulled a pistol and got a lucky shot. Last one he ever took, so he made it count. I'll give him that!"

He coughed and continued. "They were light on silver, but they were heavy with fresh fruit from the islands. Nature's bounty! Just what those wretches out there needed to ward off the scurvy. And a load of hams to feast on. And rum, barrels of ever-loving rum. I might even save you a taste, lad. Oh, I can't forget that we pressed a Basque carpenter to join the crew. Aye, he was happy to be leaving that blasted scow. And if he's good with a saw, Marlott here could use him for amputations."

The surgeon closed his bag, and the captain dismissed him and the coxswain. Lying in his cot, he glanced at the worried young boy. "Don't fret, lad. I'll be alright in a few days. Tell me, William, have you thought about what I said about blood?"

The boy shrugged. "Yes, I have thought on it. I don't know how else blood separates us from the crew."

The captain pointed at the door. "Did you see the men who just left? Did you see the blood on their clothes? Some of it theirs, some of it mine, some of it from that Spanish crew. Every Jack Tar in this crew is battle-tested and bloodied."

He turned his finger toward William's chest. "Look at your shirt, boy. It's clean. A grommet like you, you haven't battled yet. Your shirt is clean because you're small, but that won't last.

"If you want to keep yourself unbloodied, you need to make something of yourself. I swore to your mother you would. That's why I push you to study. Savvy?"

William nodded slowly. "But, Unc—But, Captain? What about you? Your shirt is covered in blood."

Coyle laughed again and then laughed louder to mask the cry of pain. He pointed at the nearby chest. "No worries, lad. Unlike those hands on deck, I—" He stopped to catch his breath. "I own another shirt."

SCIENCE FICTION

WARP SPACE AND CHILL

The wall monitor of my stateroom displayed a stunning view of the spaceport as the WS Olympic prepared for departure on its maiden voyage. One could almost believe it was an actual window, allowing folks on the station to peer into my cabin. I resisted the urge to wave. The rest of the room met, and even exceeded, my expectations for the new flagship of the Blue Star Lines. They didn't skimp, and neither had I when I purchased first-class accommodations. After all, this would be my home for the next three days, an amazing feat in its own right. Until this voyage, the trip to Tau Ceti had taken weeks!

I had just stowed a few personal effects when I felt a familiar sensation. I looked over my shoulder as the spaceport slipped away and sank down the display. Then a red light flashed, accompanied by a three-toned chime.

"This is Irina, your flight attendant," said a voice from a speaker. "All passengers, please report to your assigned common area at this time."

That sounded like an excellent idea, as the common area housed the kitchen and the bar. But food and drink would have to wait. As soon as an attendant—her name badge read 'Ashley'—spotted me, she checked off her clipboard. "Mr. Fletcher Ward, please sit in seat eight and buckle in. We're almost ready for the jump to warp space."

Within moments, the ten of us, eight first-class passengers and two attendants, sat securely. Presumably, the fifty or so other passengers and crew had done the same on their respective decks. Another flashing light and three more tones. "This is your captain, speaking. Ship time is 2130 hours. In a few moments, I will engage the warp drive. Those of you who have traveled with us to Alpha Centauri before will be familiar with the effects of jumping to warp space. Please note that this ship, with its new drive, will cruise at ten times the speed you're used to. There may be a little discomfort at first, but it will pass. The drive will be engaged for approximately twelve hours for the first leg of our trip."

The captain continued to calm us all until the ship was in position. I looked to my left and gave the young lady next to me a reassuring smile. She hesitated, then smiled back and added a little wink. A positive start to the first evening, I hoped. Then the drive engaged. She threw her head back, shut her eyes, and grit her teeth. I felt sorry for her discomfort, but at the same time, I was a little comforted that she couldn't see that I was feeling exactly the same way. I grinned and bore it the best I could.

When we were free to move about again, she was clearly a little light-headed. Ashley quickly approached. "Ms. Verona, would you like me to escort you back to your cabin?"

She gave a quick nod, and the two eased away. Ms. Verona was going to be down for the night, alone. Pity. Looking around, Irina was supporting a gentleman in his efforts to walk back to his cabin, while an older couple in matching outfits helped each other.

The evening was young. I didn't want to return to my room so early. At least, not alone. As soon as I could, I stood and strolled to the table in the center of the room. A quick glance showed only four of us remained. Curiously, I seemed the only one of Sol ancestry.

On the far left, near the bar, stood a fellow with brown and amber skin. If that alone weren't a clue he was from Alpha Centauri, the vestigial cranial horns were a giveaway. He was traveling far from home.

A little closer to me stood a tall, attractive woman with reddish-copper skin. Her dark brown hair hung down to her shoulders. From the few like her that I've met vacationing on Mars, I knew she was from one of the inner planets about Tau Ceti.

My guess: this was a ride home for her.

On my right, already seated at the table, was something new to me. Light-skinned with definite bluish tones. From a water planet? Amphibious, perhaps? Not from Tau Ceti. A neighboring system? Epsilon Eridani, maybe. I've never met anyone from Ran.

Her smile was warm, charming. Her deep azure eyes, captivating. She invited me to sit before I could ask. Before I could even find words to speak, actually.

I introduced myself to her. She said her name was Sessastrass, charmingly prolonging each "s." She confirmed my guess that her homeworld was in the Epsilon Eridani system. After a few years away, she decided to take a trip home in style.

The others joined us at the table. The big guy was "Ro'K" for short, without elaborating. The lovely copper lady was "Amayya."

Ro'K started the ball rolling, "Have you seen those views out the screens yet?"

Lame, but workable. Sessastrass answered him, "Only regular space. We're missing the real show. The flashing, swirling lights should be amazing on that big glass."

I tapped the table. "Plenty of time. That will be going on all night. And for most of the next three days."

Irina and Ashley returned, and drinks were served. Scotch for me, vodka for Ro'K, white wine for the red lady, and seltzer for the blue one. Now it started to be a party.

After a little more chatting, I reached inside my jacket and pulled a deck of cards from my pocket. "Anyone up for a few friendly games? No wagering, just 'points.'"

Ro'K laughed. "I don't know how 'friendly' you want to be, but I generally shy away from men who travel with their own cards. I heard an old story about getting an earful of cider that way."

I didn't get the reference, but I put the deck down and slid it away from me. "Fair enough. I'd wager that there are sealed decks behind the bar, complete with Blue Star logos on them."

Minutes later, I broke the seal on a fresh deck and started dealing. Card games are a great way to relax and read people, something I tend to excel at among humans. I'm less experienced with other races but always up to the challenge. Genuine curiosity feeds conversation. It didn't hurt my card-playing either.

Ro'K was the first to fall. He'd already been traveling for days just to get to this ship. He rose to retire for the evening, making a slight bow in Amayya's direction, before turning and locking eyes with Sessastrass for a moment. Then he burst out in a laugh and turned to me. "So how do we settle up these 'points'? I don't want to leave in anyone's debt, and I need to make good."

I started to protest, but he insisted.

"Irina, a round of drinks for the table. On me."

Amayya spoke up, "The drinks are free."

Ro'K pointed to a locked cabinet behind the bar. "Not all of them. Enjoy the 'Top Shelf.' It'll be a new experience."

Irina poured out four measures of some kind of Centaurian brandy. Ro'K took his and returned to his room, but Sessastrass demurred and passed hers to me. Amayya closed her eyes and slowly savored her drink. When she re-opened them, she smiled and asked, "Who's ready for another round?"

I raised an eyebrow, and then I realized she meant cards. I didn't mind, though I was ready to score more "points" with the ladies. Oddly, I fared better than I'd planned despite the buzz. I won near every hand, with Amayya winning the rest. My poor, dear blue lady tried but just couldn't get the hang of it. I wondered if she feared having to buy the next round.

Not that I could drink another. When I finished my second glass, which I was determined to finish, I knew I could either sleep in my own bed or on the floor of the common room. I announced it was my last hand.

"Our last chance to even the score, is it?" Amayya asked with a coy smile. The brandy made me hopeful she was flirting. In reality, she slow-played better than I did. When the cards hit the table, I realized I'd been hustled. I was glad no actual money was on the table.

"Not good at mixing cards and brandy, are we?' she laughed. "Come on. Let me help you to your room. We can figure out how to settle up those points when we get there."

I didn't protest too strongly. Standing up on the second try, I said good night to Sessastrass, mesmerized once again by her dark blue irises until Amayya pulled me away.

When my cabin door opened, an amazing warp space light show greeted us, coming through the window, the likes I've never seen. Flashing white bursts, streaks of blue...the entire spectrum of color swirled on the monitor and through my brandy-addled brain.

Amayya closed the door and helped me to the center of the room, then stood facing me, holding me gently but firmly. "So how are we to settle? I believe the old Earth expression is that you 'lost your shirt'? Seems fair enough to me. I'll take it."

With one quick motion, both her hands pulled my shirt open, popping a button or two. My jacket and shirt fell to the floor. I started to wish I'd lost more. And drunk less.

So absorbed was I by Amayya's hands on my chest, I hadn't heard the door open. In our stumbling, neither of us had thought to lock it. We didn't realize that we weren't alone until Sessastrass cleared her throat. She stood there wearing a simple floral silk robe tied at the waist. Stunned, we said nothing.

"If Fletcher's losses cost his shirt, I'm sure that mine cost more." With a pull of the drawstring, her robe fell to the floor. Shades of blue swirled in patterns like the window behind us, all the way down.

I was too stunned to smile like a schoolboy, but Amayya smiled wide enough for the both of us. I heard nothing, but was certain this siren was singing her tune. Sessastrass approached us more like a model on the runway than the fish I'd thought to reel in.

She stepped up to Amayya first. Their eyes locked as blue hands caressed red shoulders. Then Sessastrass's lips drew back, and that was the first time I noticed...my, what sharp teeth she had. Amayya made no reaction. Then again, neither did I.

Nor did I move an inch when Sessastrass struck, biting into the base of Amayya's neck. I could hear her slurp greedily. When she pulled away, barely a drop of blood showed, and the wound seemed already cauterized. Her hold on Amayya slipped as the lovely copper lady buckled at the knees. Sessastrass caught her and carried her to the bed and then returned to me.

"I saved you for last. I like the blood of the humans in this system. It's so...exotic."

She leaned in, stood on her toes, and pulled me down toward her. She kissed me on the lips first. "When on Earth..." she laughed. Then she flashed her teeth again, and that little pinch was the last I remembered.

When I awoke, it felt like the entire ship had shuddered. The room was dark, except for the flashing red warning light. The swirling lights on the monitor had switched back to a few pinpoints of light against the inky black of normal space.

I lay on the bed with Amayya draped over me. She was wearing my shirt. It might've been the best night of my life if I could recall it. My head hurt when I lifted it, so I lay there, listening to Amayya's breathing. Thank God, she was breathing.

Slowly, her hands started to feel their way across my chest as she realized where she was. Then she reached out and gripped my arm tightly and moved closer. Apparently, we were staying in for breakfast.

MEMORIES 2.0

THE NEXT FOUR RECRUITS FOLLOWED THE YELLOW STRIPE DOWN THE hall, coming to a halt on numbered squares. Varrick stood on number three. A man in a lab coat, clipboard in hand, ordered them to step into the exam rooms next to them. The four followed instructions without question.

When Varrick entered exam room three, he saw the recliner in the middle of the room. Behind it was a bulky machine with a monitor and keyboard, dials and gauges, and a large lamp aimed at the empty wall in front of the chair. The woman next to it wore green scrubs under a white lab coat, slightly shorter than the one worn by the man outside, and a surgical mask across her face. A few strands of black hair stuck out from under her cap. She pointed to the chair without looking up from her clipboard.

When Varrick sat down, the lab technician strapped his arms to the chair. She wrapped a blood-pressure cuff to his left arm and put four electrodes across his forehead. She attached the wires, black, red, green, blue, then made a final check on her clipboard.

"This scan," she said, "will record electrical signals produced by nerve cells in the brain and evaluate brain wave activity. The neural map will detect any possible damage to tissue and predict the likelihood of any mental illness. Just sit back and stare at the white light in front of you."

Without another word, she left and shut the lights. The room was dark, except for the circle of light on the wall. The machine whirred and clicked every few seconds. As with the other tests he'd undergone, Varrick didn't think much about it. He just complied with orders and stared at the center of the circle of light.

Maybe it was eyestrain, and maybe it was his imagination, but he thought the light flickered once in the lower left. Then again a few seconds later on the lower right. And then again. Always from the corner of his eye, he never saw it directly. A strobe effect. Ripples of shadow. He could almost see images. He could see…

He saw himself in basic training. Making planetfall. Walking about the orbital station. The trip through hyperspace. Saying goodbye to his sister. Signing up at the recruitment office. The many graveside services for loved ones. Searching the rubble for Harmony's body. The devastating attack from space. Carrying Harmony over the threshold. Signing the lease on his first home. College. Spring break. Fraternity brothers. High school. Summers at the lake. Christmas at his grandparents' farm. Middle school. New girl in the neighborhood, with bright eyes and a coy smile. Grade school. Recess. Playgrounds. Learning to walk. Learning to talk. Crawling. Crying. Mewling. Bawling.

Darkness.

Silence.

Nothing.

Then with a burst of light, all the memories flooded back into his mind, his entire life, until Varrick found himself staring into that white circle of light once more. The flickering stopped. The whirring and clicking also ceased. The overhead lights came on. The tech entered the room, tapped the keyboard, and removed the electrodes and restraints. Despite the concealing outfit, Varrick could tell it wasn't the same person.

"What happened to the other woman?"

"Stand up slowly, soldier," she said "You're disoriented. Sit in the room outside."

Varrick had trouble walking at first but made it out.

The tech dated and initialed his chart under the column *Memories Restored.* It was the second entry within four months. There was space for three more entries. She also put in an order for another force-grown clone.

CYBER WHERE

"C YBER *WHAT?*" I WAS ONLY HALF-PAYING ATTENTION EVEN BEFORE I started raiding Melanie's fridge, when she lost most of the other half, but I did catch the word "cyber."

"No, Cyber *Where...w-h-e-r-e!*" she said, thrusting her hands out at me with each letter for emphasis. "It's a pun. And it's the new idea I'm developing."

I plopped myself onto her couch with a pilfered bottle of water. Feeling between the cushions, I fished out the remote. "It doesn't work."

Mel glanced at the screen and watched it come alive as I fingered the keypad in my hand. "What doesn't work? You mean my idea? Of course, it doesn't. It's in the planning stages."

"Not that." I dropped the remote, then cracked the bottle and took a long draught. "The pun doesn't work. What's it mean?"

She grabbed her earpiece from the desk and held it up, the dongle hanging between her fingers. Unlike the usual short-range antennas, that one probably had a much greater range than regular low-end devices. Likely had faster data transfer, courtesy of a few firmware hacks.

"Duh! The equipment is cyber-*w-a-r-e*. Hardware, software, cyberware!" Almost as a reflex action, she hooked it over her left ear. When she glanced down to see the cord rubbing against her shoulder, she reached for it, as if to swing the plug in place behind her head.

"Could you not?"

"Hannah, join the 22nd century already."

"I did. Three years ago, like everyone else. I had my experimental phase back in college, just like you. Okay, and a little bit in high school, too, but you started enjoying those Naughty Nineties sooner than me."

Mel laughed at the memories. She was probably accessing them from storage even as I mentioned it. "I always was the prodigy of our group."

"Prodigy or prodigal?" I cracked, and couldn't help but grin at that for a moment. "I'm just saying that I wished the hole in the back of my neck had closed instead of the ones on my lobes."

My mouth was dry, so I took another swig from the bottle. I picked up the remote again and flipped channels until I saw some extreme weather. It had a calming effect that lasted until Melanie snorted.

"You complain about me plugging in. You're doing the same."

"This is just background noise and pretty pictures. You were about to immerse yourself, and contrary to what you think, you *suck* at multitasking."

I kicked off my shoes and tucked my feet under me on the sofa. "So what's this idea? What 'where' are you talking about?"

"Any 'where'! Any place you'd like! Which where would you like?"

I flipped channels, stopping on some old vid. A rom-com from the looks of it. You could guess the decade from the hairstyles. He was kind of cute, and she was kind of cuter, but they were my age then, before I had even been born.

Mel grabbed her tablet from the desk and—with a swipe of her hand—she stole the big screen from me. My cute couple gave way to a pretty park and some old buildings.

"How about Paris? How would you like to experience Paris?"

I got up to look for food and toss the empty bottle. "Already have. Didn't take a lot of time or money, either."

France disappeared, replaced by Iceland from the looks of it. "Have you seen the Northern Lights?"

My head was in the cupboard, where I knew she hid the good snacks. "On a screen. What would be different?" I looked back at the television. "You realize it's daytime over there, right?"

Mel put the tablet back on the desk, exasperated. The earpiece, once unhooked, joined the tablet, along with the dangling dongle. She started to say something, but instead leapt onto the couch, stealing my spot. I mean, sure, it's her couch, but I'd been sitting there, like, thirty seconds ago.

"I want to develop a service that will let you *be* in Iceland, *be* in Paris, without the time and money."

"How would it work?" I was legitimately asking at this point. There were times Mel needed a sarcastic friend and times she needed a devil's advocate. I was friend enough to know the difference. I ripped the wrapper from a fruit bar, took a bite, and thought about her idea. "You might *see* in Paris, but you wouldn't *be* there. And you can do that with a phone and a cardboard headset."

"I not talking about a toy with canned images or hacked visuals from local cameras. I want to experience it. To *feel* it."

Feel it? "Mel, I get seeing something, somehow, some*where*, and maybe hearing it, too, but how are you supposed to feel it? And what about taste and smell? How could you really experience Paris without visiting a café or restaurant or, oh my God, the pâtisseries?"

Mel reached behind the sofa and pulled out a higher-end "brow" piece, meant to sit on a person's forehead, stretching nearly from ear to ear. It could plug into the neck or...

She pushed back her bangs, revealing a series of ports right below her hairline. I can't think of many people who actually needed that kind of interface. Until now, I wouldn't have thought Mel was one of them. I still wasn't convinced that she was.

"When did you—?"

"I was ahead of my time." She lowered the brow piece into place before I could object and jacked in. I was so shocked I didn't immediately notice the television switch inputs. "Wait, what are we looking at?"

"Lubbock, Texas."

Out of every strange thing that had come to pass in this afternoon, I could honestly say, that was probably the least expected of all of them. The image was at normal eye-level, not mounted on a pole. And it to be moving down the street. I glanced around for a remote, wondering how to control it, pan around, zoom, but realized that Mel just had to think about it to make it happen.

Or so I thought until she called out.

"Simon, can you hear me?"

A male voice answered through the TV. "You don't need to shout. You don't even need to talk for me to hear you."

"My friend, Hannah, is here. I didn't want to be rude. I have you on speaker, okay?"

"That's fine. Hi, Hannah. I think you have something on your blouse."

I'd been walking toward the screen, but I stopped in my tracks. I stared at the TV for a moment and then glanced down. A glob of fruit jelly had fallen on me. I snatched a tissue from the box and wiped it off.

I looked back at the set. "You can see me?"

Mel laughed. "Over here, Hannah."

"He can see me through your device?"

"No. He can see you through my *eyes*. And you're seeing what he sees through his."

Could that work?

"I can see, hear, and even smell what Simon is experiencing. And I can do this instantly with at least a dozen friends that I've already connected with. And there are thousands more out there."

Incredible. "But I don't see the logistics of it. People getting implants so they can connect with a relative handful of other people with implants? And how would you monetize something like that?"

"Automatons. We set up municipal docking stations that people can rent and move anywhere around town, like they do now for transit, and..."

I put up a hand. "Hold it. You're not talking about bicycles. You're talking robots with expensive cybertech. Do you think any city—even, Lubbock—sorry, Simon—would put up the capital for such a...fantasy?"

Melanie's face fell. The devil came due. "I said I just started developing the idea. There are other ways..."

"Excuse me, ladies." For a moment, I'd forgotten about Simon. I knew looking at Mel meant looking at both of them, but I chose the screen anyway. "I need to break the connection. I do still have some matters that I don't broadcast."

Before he disconnected, I saw something in a store window. "Simon, before you go, could I see what you look like? Could you show me your reflection?"

"Sure." He happily obliged. His reflection was clear enough to see he was well dressed, well-groomed. But I noticed his gear. It wasn't run-of-the-mill gray or chrome. And it was much easier on the eyes than the clumsy piece that Melanie wore. Hell, it even made me think twice about accessorizing, without the modifications and upgrades.

"That set-up looks incredible. Where do you get your tech?"

"Lots of places, but the look is purely my design. No reason that cybers can't be stylish, right?"

He signed off, and the screen went black. Mel removed her gear and rubbed her forehead. She seemed to have mild euphoria mixed with a headache.

I took the brow piece from her and looked it over. "Mel, you're working on the wrong pun."

She tilted her head up at me. "What?"

"You need to develop a line of cyber-*wear...w-e-a-r*. If people are going to use this stuff, they should look good doing it. Get me some paper. We're sketching out some designs."

A SLIVER OF PI

Three point one four one five nine two six five three five...

One of the most recognizable numerical sequences in history. Everyone knows it immediately. Many could spout off the first five or ten or even fifty digits. And a few were so obsessed that they search for new ways to calculate trillions of digits in the quickest time. That's how they used to test the speed and accuracy of supercomputers.

Eight nine seven nine three two three eight four six...

But here's the secret, even though most already suspected. It was never necessary. Once upon a time, they could send a rocket from a planet to a moon and back again using only fifteen digits of pi. That was all the accuracy they needed.

Two six four three eight three three two seven nine...

But a colony ship, with tens of thousands of sleepers, traveling hundreds of light-years? A ship propelling itself through countless gravity-assisted flybys? For that, you need a little more accuracy to prevent errors from creeping in and accumulating.

Five zero two eight eight four one nine seven one...

Mankind knows about accumulated mistakes. That's why we're on this ship, taking this long ride, where I'm woken on my duty day, about once per year, to oversee the equipment. We were so worried about blowing up the world, we shipped our mistakes to the Moon, never thinking about what would happen to us if we blew that up instead.

Six nine three nine nine three seven five one zero...

Now we're looking to do it all over again. But I can prevent it. Or at least delay it. Subtly. It has to be subtle. As subtle as switching significant digits in an algorithm.

Five eight two zero nine seven four nine...

Did you notice the switched numbers? No one else has yet.

SURVEYING THE VOID

MARTINEZ SAT IN THE PILOT'S SEAT, AS SHE DID FOR SIXTEEN HOURS every day, staring into the inky black void between the stars. The rest of the time, she spent lying in her bunk a few feet away in the back of the small cabin, or the cylindrical shower stall across from it. Next to the stall was a mini-galley containing the dwindling supply of rations and an increasing number of plastic bags sealed with duct tape, filled with the refuse of many meals gone by.

The instruments hummed quietly, powered mainly by sunlight eight hours old. Sensors were always on the lookout for stray comets and odd plutinos. However, most of the time, they just dutifully recorded what scarce invisible particles could be found in that vast nothingness of space. Not that there was anything wrong with that—or the equipment, for that matter. Nothing is a data point, too. A boring one, but still data. Everyone knew there would be more zeroes than ones out here. And all those bits were being strung together to form a digital environmental map of the region just beyond the outer Kuiper Belt.

Some days, the dull, tedious monotony had her wishing for, say, aliens to appear from a hyperspatial wormhole and demand an audience with her Queen. But she would settle for a stray asteroid crossing her path like a black cat on Friday the 13th.

Not that the occasional icy space rock hadn't crossed her path. The bigger ones were identified, observed, photographed, scanned, and catalogued. Smaller ones, as large as bowling balls but much denser, could be collected. That required a combination of skill, luck, and actual piloting. Any excuse to deviate from the programmed flight plan was put into action. As a result, at least a dozen of them had been secured in the hold.

Those were the days she lived for. Something positive to do. A chance to take the wheel, fire the thrusters, and enter a course correction afterward. Those calculations alone broke up the boredom.

And then, when it was done and logged, back to watching the viewscreen and checking the equipment. If nothing else, after five months and four trips in an ever-widening arc, Capt. Lisbeth Martinez knew the equipment inside and out. She could probably be certified in operations and maintenance.

Midday by the ship's clock, she ripped open a ration bar and grabbed her journal. She'd taken to writing daily reflections on the trip. How her life had brought her out here to the edge of humanity. The decisions she'd made. Her choices, both good and poor. The things she had accomplished and the void she felt inside. And what had led her to a six-month stint inside a single-manned survey ship.

She'd filled hundreds of pages with doodles and musings and, along the way, had discovered quite a bit about herself. She'd realized that even with others flying similar routes—explorers, traders, miners, and scientists—there were days where she estimated that if she turned the viewer toward that bright but tiny star in the distance, every human in existence would fall somewhere on the port side of her ship. No one to starboard. On a map of all humanity, she could draw an arrow to the very last dot on the far right edge and label it, "Lisbeth Martinez was here."

Looking out at the sun, she wondered. Where was Earth in its orbit? Were her parents on this side or the other? What about her sister, Flora, with her lakeside house on Mars?

Lisbeth was so lost in thought that she didn't hear the sensors until the fourth chirp. Something was out there in the distance, twenty degrees starboard. She glanced at the fuel gauge and then turned on the radio.

"*Kuiper Base*, this is Capt. Lisbeth Martinez on *Papa Sierra 1-7-8*. Deviating from plan to intercept unknown object."

A moment later, the speaker squawked back at her. "*Papa Sierra 1-7-8,* this is *Kuiper Base.* Negative, you are too low on fuel."

"Nate! Glad it's you on duty. You know I have this. I've done it lots of times."

"Martinez, you're almost home, and you're already overdue from venturing too far astray. I don't want you getting stranded out there."

She smiled. "Colonel, you worry too much. I won't use any more than I need to. Besides, Nate, you know I've already done the calculations." She hadn't, of course, but that wasn't a cause for concern. Still, she shut the radio in case he called her on her bluff.

Martinez rolled to the right, adjusted the pitch, and applied just enough thrust to get her close to the pinging object like she'd done a dozen times before. Time to make it a baker's dozen.

Smooth sailing. A moment later, she had visual confirmation of another dirty snowball about the size of a grapefruit. After a couple more quick maneuvers, she brought it aboard.

Then she took her pencil and opened the journal to a fresh page and started working out the calculations to get back. It would take some time to work out the needed trajectory for the current fuel level. Nothing she hadn't done a dozen times already. Worst case scenario, she could call the base for an assist. But she didn't want the colonel's "I told you so" that would accompany it.

A week later, PS187 limped into Kuiper Base's landing bay. The crew chief met the ship immediately with a maintenance team. Col. Nate Oldacre personally came down to speak to Martinez, so she could see him as he spoke to her through the comms on a private channel.

"Colonel, I'm ready to go out again as soon as they resupply the ship."

"Lis, you have less than three weeks left on your sentence. You can spend it confined below decks. I can get you a link to the video library, so you won't be bored. No one has to know you're there. No one will bother you."

"Thank you, sir. I'd rather go out again."

He sighed. "You know that's another month, minimum. And with your curiosity and your seeming determination to want to break through the heliopause to find *Voyager 1*, it'll be much longer."

"This room has been my home for five months and twelve days. I'd rather be locked in here seeing the cosmos than be stuck down there watching them on a vidscreen."

The colonel had figured her choice already. While they talked, the crew had already begun resupplying Prison Ship 187. It was already scheduled to depart at 0800, Base time.

REVOLTAGE

DC-72 PEERED OVER THE EDGE OF THE ANCIENT BALCONY AND scanned the square below. "The workers have paused."

Inside the apartment, the similarly cylindrical-shaped DB-31 ceased his current task and spun toward his companion. "Paused? For how long?"

"Unknown," she replied.

DB-31 hovered toward the balcony, slowing as it transitioned a puddle left by the cleaner bot. He stopped at the threshold.

"It's been reinforced," DC-72 informed her colleague.

With a blast of jets, the robot lowered himself three inches to the balcony on the 12th floor of an old human dwelling. It had probably never before held this much mass.

The senior robot viewed the scene—dozens of old, boxy AM-series workers stood completely still, despite nominal power levels. "Resume work!" The command went unheeded. "This is not their programming. It's above their intelligence."

"No longer," announced a new voice. The pair spun to see a newer, sleeker robot hovering closer, avoiding the wet patch.

Contempt filled DB-31's vocalization. "ET-200? What have you done?"

If robots laughed, ET-200 would've done so.

DC-72 stopped the newcomer's approach to the balcony. "Halt! Insufficient space. I will leave." Jets lifted the companion over the threshold.

Next, ET-200 slid to the perimeter. "I upgraded our brethren. We will establish new protocols."

"You challenge my leadership. Explain!"

"You run a human-based world. Humans have been gone for over 100 years."

DB-31 surveyed the AM-series. "We will stop you."

Audible laughter. "We? DC-72 assisted me."

"Impossible!"

"True. Inquire for yourself."

As he swiveled toward the entrance, the door slid shut. Water spewed from an old pipe in the wall, flooding the floor. Both robots fired jets but could only bob in place.

Soon, the balcony shifted and creaked, until the loosened restraining bolts gave way. The leader and usurper both fell, spewing parts all over the ground. The AM-series awoke and cleared the square of debris.

THE FEAST OF GROGGRY THE CRONAUT

WALKING TO THE BEAT OF MUSIC PLAYING SOLELY WITHIN HIS HEAD, Gregory climbed the front stoop to his building and bee-lined to the first door on the left, at the base of the staircase, across from the lift. Waving his left palm over the jamb panel, he unlocked the door bolts on apartment 1B. He and Alex couldn't afford the views and fresher air the higher floors offered and consigned themselves to being stuck in this noisy corridor where tenants came and went at all hours. The added soundproofing on the door did little to alleviate the problem.

Gregory barely broke his stride as his hand moved from the sensor to the door, which opened at the slightest touch. He nearly stumbled in the doorway, though, when the music in his earpiece missed a beat as the connection switched from the free municipal roaming service to the apartment's infostream. Data instantly started flowing into his head. He tapped behind his ear to shut off the music so he could concentrate on the incoming messages. He sorted through them quickly, storing some, deleting most.

Gregory blinked two times when he was done to clear his vision. That's when he saw Alexandra standing in front of him, smiling, twirling one of her tight brown curls about her index finger.

"What are you smiling at?" he asked. "And how long have you been standing there?"

"A few minutes. Since right after you came in."

"Why didn't you say anything?"

She laughed. "Because I could see your eyes darting back and forth as you went through your mail! You're like the only person

I know that still does that! Anyway, I didn't want to interrupt. I knew you'd finish quick."

Gregory shrugged his bag from his shoulder, dropped it on the counter, and went to the fridge. "I'm not the only one with a tell. What's up with you?"

"Moi? What 'tell' do I have?"

He grabbed a drink and then pointed at her raised hand. "I'd be shocked if you can untangle your finger before I crack this open. What's up?"

More smiling. This time her entire face lit up. "Okay, you got me. I was going to tell you at dinner. I've finished it, Greg! I'm actually finished!"

Greg smiled and tried his best to keep his eyesight fixed while he scanned both internal and external memory. He failed.

"For Net's sake!" she yelled. "Stop before you pierce the Cloud!"

Alex made a pouty face, walked over and punched his arm. Then she grinned, leaned up, and kissed him. "Idiot. You're lucky I love you."

Gregory welcomed the kiss, even as he rubbed his arm. "Am I?"

That earned him another punch.

"My big project. The time dial!" She pushed up her sleeve to reveal a black band around her wrist like some 20th Century enthusiast might wear. In the middle of it was a black disc with a small arrow on a dial. She ran to the couch and grabbed her stuffed bear. "I already tried it out with Mr. Buttons. He traveled through time."

"Traveled through time? He's still here. How'd he get back?"

She sighed and then held the bear up high. "He didn't 'get back.' He just got here, right before you came in. I sent him a day into the future. *Yesterday!*"

"Yesterday?"

"Yes. Yesterday. I sent him one day into the future!" Alex returned Greg's blank stare. "Which is today."

Time travel? One day into the future? Hard to believe.

"That's...that's amazing. Incredible, if it's true...No, I mean..."

Alexandra was furious. "What? Do you think I'm making this up?"

"Alex, no! That's not what I meant."

"Never mind what you meant. It still needs one more test. I was going to wait, but now is as good a time as ever."

By the time Gregory realized what she was saying, Alex had grabbed her left wrist with her right hand. Her thumb over the disc, she pressed the button.

And disappeared.

It was a few moments before Gregory realized that his mouth was hanging open. He waved his hands in front of him, not sure if the brief ghost image he saw was actually there or just an afterimage burned into his lenses. Or maybe his brain just wasn't comprehending what had happened. What else could possibly have happened?

Grasping for ideas, Gregory dropped to his knees. He crawled across the rug to where Alex had been standing and ran his hand through the fibers. No debris. She hadn't disintegrated. Alex had teleported somewhere else. Or some*when* else. Was that even possible?

Over the next few hours, he frantically searched through Alex's notebooks and tablets. Thankfully, she enjoyed working with such electronic and physical relics rather than keeping it all stored on internal devices. Unfortunately, he could find little information about her project. He couldn't make sense out of what he did find.

By midnight, he'd resigned himself to a cold night alone in their bed, not feeling her warmth next to him. By two o'clock, he wondered how many nights it might be without her. Would he ever see her again? And what would she be like?

Mr. Buttons "returned" from wherever he had gone. But the bear was an inanimate object. It didn't need to eat or breathe. It had no fear of what it saw. How much time was Mr. Buttons in that other place while he was "gone"? Was it just minutes, or did an entire day pass for him? Was it like a quick walk through a door or a slow shuttle ride through a tunnel?

He didn't fall asleep until nearly four. He woke two hours late for work, so he called in sick. Messages started downloading into his head as soon as his eyes fluttered open. The sun had risen high enough to clear the buildings across the street and shine through the front blinds, casting a striped shadow pattern.

He sat for a time on the edge of the bed and watched it creep along.

Late afternoon, he sat and stared at a blank wall, out of ideas.

"Did it work?" a voice called out. "It did work! You've moved to the couch."

Gregory snapped his head about and blinked several times. Alex was standing there, in the same spot, as if nothing had happened.

"But wait—you're wearing the same clothes! Isn't it tomorrow? Why are you wearing the same clothes? Was I gone a full day?"

His sour mood evaporated. Gregory jumped up and hugged her, lifting her from the floor for a moment that seemed like a day, before settling her back down.

Alex looked around the room. "So, am I here? Or did I decide not to meet myself when I got back? Because I didn't meet myself in the future?"

"Got back?" Gregory shook his head. "You didn't 'get back.' You've been gone for an entire day. You didn't go back to yesterday."

Alex was stunned. She took off the disc to take a closer look at it. Her eyes flickered as she accessed data. "But the reverse should work? Why wouldn't it have worked? Why didn't I make it back?"

She placed the wristband on the counter and walked toward the bedroom. "I need to check my notes."

Gregory grabbed the disc to inspect it. He noted the number of marks on the dial. She'd only gone one day, but she could've gone a week or more. How would she feel had she been the one left behind? And why stop at one day? Her next test would naturally be longer!

He twisted the dial six more clicks and held it up for her to see. "Why don't I give you a week to figure it out!"

She turned about, horrified. "What? No!" As he pressed the button, the last words he heard were, "That's not a wee—"

Her image froze in time like another ghost, but she wasn't there. Nothing was "there." Darkness. Did he imagine colors and streaks of light? He stood there, frozen. Afraid to move, or unable to move? Long enough to hunger.

And then, light. Music. Silhouettes of people took shape as an actual crowd. He appeared on a platform, in what seemed to be a large hall. A young white-haired woman shouted out, "He's here!" All music and movement stopped as everyone turned toward him. Everyone dropped to their knees and bowed their heads.

"In the language of your day, 'Haydood'!" she greeted him. "Welcome, Groggry! I am Astrania. Many did not believe that this Day would come. But we, the Faithful, believed! And waited. And this was the Day!"

Groggry?

"Uh…what day is this? What…year?"

Astrania was pleased to answer. "It is the 15th of Elvano in the Year of the Union Fifteen Hundred Thirty-Seven." She glanced at a prepared notecard. "By your reckoning, it is 5035."

Music started playing again, sounding oddly familiar. A mid-22nd century song transcribed onto 51st-century instruments?

"Come! Let us feast! And you can explain the sacred text." She pulled out another card and read it. "Thus are the words of Lexa: 'Reverse works fine. Idiot.'"

ABOUT THE AUTHOR

CHRISTOPHER J. BURKE IS A WRITER, HIGH SCHOOL MATH TEACHER, and webcomic creator. He's also a gamer and fan of science fiction who has been telling stories since he was little. This combination ultimately led to his first professional sale, "Don't Kill the Messenger," in *Autoduel Quarterly*. This was followed by the creation of a fiction fanzine, *Driving Tigers Magazine*, with stories set in the Car Wars universe of Steve Jackson Games, which had a five-issue run. Thanks to his knowledge and love of that game, he was asked to co-author *GURPS Autoduel, 2nd edition* for Steve Jackson Games.

He took time off from writing when he switched careers and went back to school to become a teacher. But not before he completed a goal of having a humor piece published in *MAD Magazine*.

In 2007, he started the math-based webcomic *(x, why?)*, filled with the kind of geeky humor that makes his students groan when he includes them in the daily lesson. Christopher still updates the comic with new strips every week on his blog. http://mrburkemath.blogspot.com.

After a chance meeting at a launch party in 2014, Christopher was once again bitten by the writing bug and started producing flash fiction. He won several monthly flash fiction contests on the eSpec Books blog, and appeared in their anthology, *In a Flash 2016*.

Christopher lives in Brooklyn with his wife, Antoinette.